A Land Without Jasmine

A Land Without Jasmine

Wajdi al-Ahdal

Translated by William Maynard Hutchins

A Land Without Jasmine

Published by
Garnet Publishing Limited
8 Southern Court
South Street
Reading
RG1 4QS
UK

www.garnetpublishing.co.uk
www.twitter.com/Garnetpub
www.facebook.com/Garnetpub
garnetpub.wordpress.com

First Edition

ISBN: 978-1-85964-310-5

British Library Cataloguing-in-Publication Data
A catalogue record for this book is available from the British Library

Typeset by Samantha Barden
Jacket design by Haleh Darabi

Printed and bound in Lebanon by International Press:
interpress@int-press.com

To you who are without flaw I will explain this as well: that it is the most secret wisdom and the supreme form of knowledge that allows you to attain ultimate perfection.

The Bhagavad Gita

Contents

About the Author

Wajdi Muhammad Abduh al-Ahdal is a Yemeni novelist, short story writer, screenwriter and dramatist. Born in 1973, he received a degree in literature from Sanaa University. He won the Afif prize for a short story in 1997, a gold medal for a dramatic text in the Festival for Arab Youth in Alexandria, Egypt in 1998 and the youth prize of the President of the Republic of Yemen for a short story in 1999. He is currently employed in Dar al-Kutub, the National Library in Sanaa.

He has published several collections of short stories: *Zahrat al-Abir* (The Passerby's Flower, Sanaa, 1997), *Surat al-Battal* (Portrait of an Unemployed Man, Amman, 1998), *Ratanat al-Zaman al-Miqmaq* (Gibberish in a Time of Ventriloquism, Sanaa, 1998) and *Harb lam Ya'alam bi-Wuqu'iha Ahad* (A War No One Knew About, Sanaa, 2001). His novels are: *Qawarib Jabaliya* (Mountain Boats, Beirut, 2002), *Himar Bayna al-Aghani* (A Donkey Among the Songs or A Donkey in the Choir, Beirut 2004), *Faylasuf al-Kurantina* (Quarantine Philosopher, Sanaa, 2007) and *Bilad bila Sama* (A Land Without Sama [or a Sky], published here as A Land Without Jasmine, Sanaa, 2008). His screenplay *al-Ughniya al-Mashura* (The Enchanted Song) was published in Sanaa in 2006 and his play *al-Suqut min Shurfat al-'Alam* (Falling off the Balcony of the World) was published in Sanaa in 2007.

Al-Ahdal's novel *Mountain Boats* proved controversial. An extremist campaign against the book drove him into exile and the book's publisher faced charges. When the German Nobel Laureate Günter Grass visited Yemen in December 2002 for a cultural conference, he was received by the Yemeni President Ali Abdullah Saleh to whom he mentioned al-Ahdal's situation and asked the President to protect him. Al-Ahdal was then allowed to return to his country. *Himar bayna al-Aghani* is dedicated to Günter Grass in appreciation. Although al-Ahdal's passport was seized at Sanaa Airport in the spring of 2010 he was later allowed to travel.

Note from the Translator

For this translation I started with the 2008 Sanaa edition published by by Markaz Ibadi lil-Dirasat wa-l-Nashr. I then checked my translation against the author's computer file and added three sexually explicit passages that had been deleted from the published version.

Chapters 1 and 2 appeared in a slightly different form in *Banipal Magazine* 36, Autumn/Winter 2009, pp. 178–199.

William Maynard Hutchins, 2012

1
The Queen

When I enter the bathroom first thing in the morning I feel uncertain and anxious. I start to examine myself in the mirror while my fingers probe my feet, belly, chest and head. Then I shudder involuntarily. Once I'm sure that I haven't lost any of my body I praise God and sigh with relief. Returning to my senses I realize I've merely had a beautiful, harmless, enjoyable dream, one of those delightful dreams when a girl sees herself as a bride on her wedding night.

After drying my face with my rose-coloured towel, I head towards the curtains, which I draw back. I enjoy looking out of the window, gazing at the joyous colours of the sky shortly before sunrise.

My name is Jasmine Nashir al-Ni'am. I'm a first year student in the Faculty of Science and my hobbies are reading, and writing in my diary.

My room, which is on the second floor, overlooks a quiet back street. Opposite, down below, is Hajj Sultan's grocery store. This man, even though he's made the pilgrimage to Mecca, when he sees me peek out of the window, stands there smiling idiotically and makes an obscene gesture. He puts his large store key in his ear, moving it in and out while his eyes flash fiendishly. Then I can't resist running to the bathroom to fetch a slipper to brandish at him.

He's fifty, as old as my father, and short and stout with a grey beard and a prayer callus on his forehead. Instead of growing angry and indignant he winks at me and I see him nod his head cheerfully as if confident he'll get me some day!

I slip into a black coat and veil my face before heading out. Behind his door's peep-hole, Ali, the adolescent son of our neighbours, whose apartment faces ours, has been lying in wait for me. The moment he sees me descend the stairs he pursues me like my shadow, clutching his books, which are wrapped in a prayer rug, under his arm.

His secondary school is in the same direction as my faculty but further. It takes him twenty minutes walking at a fast clip to reach it before the bell rings and the gate closes. Ali is sixteen, four years my junior. He is tall and good-looking, and his skin is fair, smooth and sleek. His body ripples with flesh and fat, and his protruding butt gives him a feminine allure that troubles me and makes him a target for lewd sexual advances from men.

During the ten minutes that he shadows me he doesn't say a word and doesn't even hum a tune. All I hear is the rapid shuffle of his feet behind me. But I sense that his ardent glances are devouring my buttocks. I feel as if fiery rays are striking them, almost melting them.

The way this taciturn boy looks at me upsets me. Occasionally he focuses on me so intently I grow hot and tremble. Then I panic and perspire. I feel so upset my steps become clumsy and one leg brushes against the other.

People's curious stares dog celebrities, who avoid appearing in public places for this reason. In Yemen, all young women are considered celebrities! When a girl leaves her home and ventures onto the street she'll notice that everyone is staring at her. Perhaps some girls feel good when men look lustfully at them but this continuous gaze from dozens of passers-by upsets me, gets on my nerves and makes me feel unbearably tense.

I consider this mass gaze, which comes from all directions, to be a noxious type of male violence. It's true their stare isn't tangible and that it's not like being touched by a hand but it exerts psychological pressure, tightens my chest and makes it hard to breathe. This gaze by repressed males assaults my skin, makes my blood boil and scrambles my thinking.

As an experiment, I once stared straight into a cat's eyes. He fled in alarm, his tail between his legs! Whenever I want to vent my rage at the male gaze I stare into the eyes of cats. This disconcerts them and they invariably flee. All cats are uneasy when someone gazes into their eyes; they assume he intends to harm them.

My grandfather told me that when he was young he left his mountain village one night and passed through a dense forest where he encountered a leopard blocking the narrow rocky trail. He shone his torch at the animal and fixed his gaze on its eyes, which glowed like embers. He stood there resolutely looking at it. Do you know what happened next? My grandfather said the leopard was visibly troubled; felt perplexed and sensed danger. It turned tail and disappeared back to its lair in the forest.

My late grandfather repeatedly told me about this incident because he wanted me to know how to react when confronting a leopard. But his story hasn't ever helped me since leopards are extinct in Yemen. Besides, I live in a city where it's inconceivable that leopards would appear on the street. What I gained from my grandfather's story was that even leopards, those prime predators, lose courage and turn tail when a person stares resolutely into their eyes. If a leopard can't think straight when only one person stares at him, what about my state of mind when dozens of men are staring at me simultaneously?

On the street most men look at me lecherously and all of them want to screw me. If they weren't also watching each other I'd be raped on the pavement at least twenty times a day. Is it because I'm unmarried and have never had any sexual adventures that I seem so extraordinarily committed to virtue? Occasionally I reflect that if I were to experiment by closeting myself with a member of the rougher sex I might then feel differently about the male gaze.

I've nothing against sex. In fact, I await with bated breath my bridegroom's arrival. But this overly intense, ocular male provocation enrages me, almost driving me crazy at times. Then I must exert a superhuman effort to keep myself from screaming and cursing.

Who knows? Perhaps I'll change once I've married and be like my faculty classmate Nasama, who is delighted when men ogle her!

Men in our country are secular in their own special way, making a clear distinction between mosque and daily life! In the mosque our men pray devoutly and piously, embodying such praiseworthy characteristics that they seem to be Merciful God's angels. But the moment they're back on the street they forget God, morph into evil demons, practise duplicity, deceit and perfidy, and chase after forbidden pleasures. I've seen a white-haired man in his seventies emerge from the mosque, his shoes still in his hand, and ogle me while licking his chops as if he wanted to nip me with his decaying teeth.

I would strongly advise any girl in my country against carrying a white handbag because this colour attracts men's attention in a weird way. Some men succumb to a special type of hysteria known as 'White Handbag Hysteria' in which the victim loses control of his senses and of himself. I witnessed an instance of this syndrome myself the only time I carried a white bag. That was the most miserable day of my life!

It happened as I walked past a construction site where labourers were carrying bags of cement on their backs into a new building. A worker with rippling muscles caught sight of me, heaved the bag of cement off his back and began to yell right in my face: 'Have mercy on me, Lord of the White Bag ... have mercy!' I froze in alarm and nearly wet my knickers I was so terrified by his hungry look!

His fellow workers and even passers-by froze like statues and I saw him rub his crotch while he continued his monstrous, bestial howl as spittle ran from both sides of his mouth: 'O Lord of the White Bag … White!' I crossed to the far side of the street and started to walk faster, feeling that my honour had been defiled, my femininity violated and my virtue sullied.

In our city it's not considered wrong to pee in the street. In fact, it's an everyday event! So I see a lot of men urinate standing up, and notice that the vicious ones deliberately display their hosepipe when a pretty girl passes, pretending they are peeing. I occasionally sneak a peek, curious to see their fountains, but the acrid smell sends a shudder of disgust through my entire body.

I'm harassed many times a day. When I hand the bus driver the fare he will deliberately push his talons in between my fingers and only take the fare after having enjoyed touching me. I'm not a devout girl and that's why I used to ignore these fleeting touches, thinking them a kind of tax exacted from every girl who ventures out on our repressed streets. But one young bus driver with an ugly face and a ruddy complexion made me change my views; now I object to this paltry gender tax. I've started to toss the coin onto the dashboard, even though people may say I'm stuck-up or that I pay the fare in a humiliating way.

This young man, who had repulsive features and hair that came down to his shoulders, was overflowing with health and vigour. I'll never forget him as long as I live; when I was last to leave the bus and held out my hand to give him the money he stuck his claws into my flesh up to the wrist, grasping my hand in his huge paw. I felt him quiver as if an electric current had shocked him. He moaned and leaned forward in delight as he released a dreadful groan of pain. I pulled my hand away in alarm and walked about aimlessly, forgetting the way home. My head was whirling around in a vortex and my feet were unsteady. Even today I don't know why I was so afraid of that driver; it's an irrational fear that I experience but can't explain.

Even though I'm very cautious, protect my personal space and take care to avoid getting too close to men, they not only touch my body, they ... If it weren't for my disgust over the experiences I've had I'd recount them in detail.

One incident that has stuck in my memory and that still elicits my intense disgust is the time I went to the market with our neighbour Umm Ali. She was leaning over to inspect some nightshirts that an itinerant vendor had spread out on the sidewalk when a man, whose moustache covered half his face, passed behind her with his thumb raised. I watched what happened next with astonishment. He continued on his way, not blinking, his features immobile, while she straightened up with the coquetry of a young filly and turned toward him laughing.

Will I share her feelings when I'm her age? Will I laugh at a man who flirts with me in this crude way?

When I was seven I thought of killing myself by plunging the kitchen knife into my belly. Then I could die an innocent child without sin and enter paradise immediately.

The world of grownups used to keep me awake at night, especially the feverish sexual atmosphere in which they lived. In my early years I felt a terrifying loathing for the way adults fall apart over sex. I had learned from books and from relatives that grownups must have sex exactly the way children must eat and drink. I decided to spare myself this inevitable sexual destiny by killing myself. I went into the kitchen and stuck the knife into my belly as I wept hot, bitter tears. With the passing years the thought of suicide has receded.

During my childhood I considered sex so vile that it should be forbidden, even to spouses. That's why I hated my father and mother because I knew that their relationship wasn't pure and that they did things in secret that weren't innocent.

I adopted moral views that were quite prim and didn't tolerate human desires; as I conceived it, the ideal world would lack any and all forms of sexual attraction. Now that I've grown up and understand life I've learned to tolerate conjugal sex. In fact, I think it's necessary so that progeny will continue to be produced.

In my childhood I went through a phase when I thought I should avoid the world of pleasures but the desires I feel now make me scoff at the naiveté of the child I used to be and at her way of thinking about these things. The transformations that our ethical principles undergo are really strange!

At home I have to put up with my eldest brother's covert attempts to read my diary. He suspects that love may have found its way into my heart. Ever since I enrolled at the university, where instruction is co-ed, he has been searching my papers for my hypothetical boyfriend. There's nothing in my diary for me to be ashamed of because although I don't brag about it I'm a paragon of virtue.

My father, for his part, is also plagued by doubts about me. I can tell he says to himself when he scans my eyes, 'The mature female searches for a mate!' Ever since I became a young woman and my breasts developed he has been prejudiced against me and apprehensive, fearing that I will sully his honour, disgrace him and besmirch his reputation.

Whenever he enters or leaves our building he always stares at my window. He feels qualms about my conduct and suspects me of standing behind the windowpane to flirt with young men. I have explained to him repeatedly that, during the day, passers-by really can't see through the glass, but he doesn't believe me at all. In his heart of hearts he believes that women's wiles are formidable. My father has become my adversary and is openly hostile to me because I haven't married yet and still live in his home. He considers me a landmine that will explode beneath his feet at any moment if he neglects to supervise me.

Even my mother, who is the one person in the world closest to my heart, stares at my face intensely when I return from the university, searching for any trace of love. I realize that she hugs me on my return so she can smell my clothing and make sure I don't bear the scent of any unknown billy-goat.

Every day she raises the same subject with me, 'What did you do today?' and interrogates me about my relationships with male professors and classmates in the faculty. Her heightened anxiety distresses me but in spite of everything I forgive her and love her.

My life is nonstop suffering on account of the stares directed at me all the time, both inside our house and out. I'm under supervision night and day. No one thinks about me, about my feelings, dreams and ambitions, or concedes that I have a right to live at ease without anyone troubling me with his inquisitive gaze and repressed desires, and a right to a happy life that a father should not poison with his suspicions and fantasies or a mother by poking her nose into my private affairs.

I feel that I'm under siege, that my society assails me from every direction and that I must have committed some unknown crime against them thousands of years ago, a crime no one bothered to record, even though it still reverberates in their unconscious. When a girl matures she certainly counts as society's number one enemy!

I don't hate anyone, not even my society, but everyone around me makes me feel that I'm not a human being with a brain and a spirit but merely an instrument of pleasure. They've compressed my human existence into a small, dirty triangle, ignoring all the rest of me. This terrifying struggle is over a putrid piece of meat! Bug off! Take this piece of meat and let me live in peace.

2
The Minion of Pleasure and Power

At 1 a.m. I received a missing person's report on a girl of twenty.

My name is Abdurrabbih Ubayd al-Adini and I'm an inspector in Criminal Investigations.

I received her description and a colour photo taken six months ago. We pulled that from her folder at the University Records Office. We didn't find any recent pictures of her in the family's photo album. They only had pictures of her as a child. (That's odd, isn't it?)

Her father, Nashir al-Ni'am, didn't provide me with any useful information. He was in a state of extreme, fiery agitation and sparks flew from his eyes as if he were a ferocious lion. He cursed everyone he could think of: he cursed his missing daughter, he cursed young men, calling them 'Tyros and …', he cursed the state and the police, he cursed his children and his wife. He even bestowed a dozen vile epithets on me, too.

Never in my entire life have I seen a face change colour from one minute to the next the way Hajj Nashir al-Ni'am's did. While he was speaking, his face would turn red and swell up till I thought, from the intense way he was holding his breath and venting his rage, that if I pierced his cheek with my fingernails, blood would splatter all over me and the walls.

When he listened to me and my fellow officers his face lost its colour, turning dull and dark, as if he were a murderer chained to his cage in the courtroom while waiting for the judges to pronounce the verdict. When we were silent and he was swept up in his private world, seeing in his mind's eye his daughter's honour being defiled, the blood drained from his face and he became alarmingly pale. His skin turned so grey it was pitiful, and I feared at those moments that he was suffering from angina.

I could call Jasmine's mother 'The Lady of the Vale of Tears'; her eyes were as red as embers and her eyelids had become inflamed from weeping. She slapped her cheeks the whole time, grieving for her daughter and blaming herself. She'll probably go crazy if her Jasmine doesn't return soon. Instead of giving me any useful information, she knelt at my feet, kissed my knees and begged me to bring her daughter back. By the time I left her I was sighing with frustration; these people who wanted me to find their daughter had been no help at all.

According to the information I had, Jasmine had left home at 7.30 that morning on her way to the university and hadn't returned. We undertook a thorough investigation of the Faculty of Science, where her classmates, male and female, confirmed that on this ill-omened morning she had attended Dr. Aqlan's lecture, which had lasted from 8 to 10 a.m. No one had seen her after she quit the lecture hall.

A hunch led me to the office of Dr. Aqlan, whose original name was said to be the less elegant 'Ajlan'. I was told he had changed his name on receiving his doctorate. I had a number of questions for him.

I asked, 'What do you think of your student Jasmine?'

He responded cautiously, 'In what respect?'

I laughed and said sarcastically, 'Any you want.'

Raising one eyebrow he said, 'Jasmine is a below average student. In her first term she received low marks in my subject.'

A student wanted to come into the office but Dr. Aqlan waved him away.

Studying his features, the proportions of his clean-shaven face, his hair, which was dyed black, and his large ears, I realized that he was a ladies' man, an indefatigable lothario.

So I lowered my voice and asked, 'What do you think of her morals?'

He wasn't surprised. He had been expecting my question and answered through pursed lips, 'She's a loose girl who claims virtue, though virtue claims her not. She makes a show of being pious and devout while actually she's the reverse.'

I was shocked by his comments, by his accusations, which were honed like the blade of a knife. Straightening in my seat I asked coldly, 'How do you know she's ... I mean ... not of good character?'

He smiled cunningly and his jaw dropped like a wolf's muzzle as he remarked, 'I'm an observant man and have spiritual insights. I can deduce mankind's secret thoughts from one simple gesture and ...'

I interrupted him curtly: 'Excuse me; my question is how you know she's a loose girl?'

He scowled and his expression grew sullen. His deceptive veil was drawn back and he hissed in a low voice, 'Two weeks ago I went into the laboratory to run a class with a co-ed group of students. Wanting to break down the psychological barrier between us I greeted them and proceeded to shake hands. When I held my hand out to her she apologized, saying that she didn't shake hands with men. She left my hand hanging in the air and put me in a ludicrous situation. I heard some male students laugh at me. That's how I discovered that she's one of these women who pretend to be modest and who refuse to shake hands in public but then open their cunts in private. This type of feminine hypocrisy is widespread. You find that such a woman always does the opposite of what she advocates and says the reverse of what she believes in her heart. It's a putrid type raised in a rotten way and living a life of contradictions. To be candid, this girl has a split personality and is two-faced.'

I put an end to his foolish prattle and said, as I looked him straight in the eye, 'Dr. Aqlan, let's speak candidly. It's possible that Jasmine may have fallen in love with one of her classmates and gone off with him; perhaps she's simply eloped with him. What do you think?'

He wagged his head and fingered his earlobe. After some reflection he replied, 'This is not too likely. We are a conservative society.'

Just then he blinked and I sensed that he wasn't satisfied with his response. I pressed him harder, 'Have you noticed whether any of your male students are interested in her?'

He narrowed his eyes and looked at me intently as he began to consider various possibilities. After he had remained silent for a long time I prodded him, 'What's his name?'

He replied slowly, 'I don't know.'

We were silent for a while, and he seemed to be reviewing specific memories till he forgot I was there. A sudden thought took hold of me with growing insistence. Following my hunch I asked him, 'Does your wife live with you?'

As if returning from the depths of the oceans he replied, 'No, she's in the village.'

I pulled out a pack of cigarettes and lit one. When I blew smoke in his face, he reacted by raising his brows. Then he asked me coldly, 'Why do you ask about my wife? What bearing does she have on the topic?'

I gazed up at the ceiling, from which the paint was peeling, and said, 'I don't know. It just crossed my mind to ask.'

'You're lying,' he retorted loudly, betraying his anger. 'You suspect me.'

Noting the agitated tapping of his feet I replied, 'Your previous statement revealed your interest in her.'

He recoiled in dismay and glared at me with venomous hatred. He looked at his watch and opened his mouth as if trying to say something; but he was unable to get out a single syllable. Then he grabbed his black briefcase and departed.

I recorded a number of observations about him in my notebook and decided to concentrate my investigations on him. I would find out what he had done the previous day and would place his apartment under surveillance.

At this point he wasn't a suspect, but my hunch, which was based on years of experience as an interrogator, was that he wasn't telling everything he knew. The way he spoke about her confirmed that there was something between them. The question about his wife had simply been a ruse to unnerve him and cause him to spill the beans about someone else.

At 1 p.m. I received a report on Jasmine from the Bureau of Investigations: 'There is no record of her in the hospitals or police stations. Her whereabouts are unknown.'

I lunched in a salad bar and had some tea in an empty café while devising an excellent plan for investigating the more murky aspects of Jasmine's disappearance.

I strongly suspected she might have been lured somewhere and held against her will. In cases like this time is of the essence. If she hadn't been killed already her life was now in extreme danger. I went back to her family's residence and at the door to the building found a crowd of her relatives, some armed with Kalashnikov rifles. They were arguing vociferously with each other, all wound up and ready to explode.

I mingled with them and they began to ask me loutishly about their missing relative. Their faces were terrifying, so angry that they spewed ill will, and their eyes glowed with savagery, like those of angry lions. Jasmine is a member of a particularly ferocious tribe; all its men are heroic warriors for whom a daughter's honour is the red line; any creature crossing that line is destined to die.

I heard them threaten her father that if they found Jasmine and she was no longer a virgin, a thousand bullets would rip through her body. This totally threw me; I could no longer distinguish one thing from another, and I forgot the plan I had prepared.

The tribe's shaykh arrived in a late-model sedan that bristled with armed men. He stepped out haughtily and majestically, encircled by guards on every side, and the men of the tribe clustered around him. I wasn't able to approach because of all the crowding and shoving. So I stood on a stone bench in the distance to watch what was happening. I saw Jasmine's father grovel so humbly before the shaykh that his abasement could well have killed him as his head struck the ground.

Over our heads a kite screeched as it circled low. I felt depressed and my senses seemed strangely disturbed. I realized that fear from some unknown source had wormed its way into my soul and that a chill was spreading through my bones.

The venerable shaykh issued his directives calmly and gravely. Then he climbed back into his superb sedan – as his guards elbowed each other for pride of place, leaping into the rear seats – and left the neighbourhood as swiftly as he had appeared.

I no longer had control of the situation and was in a pitiful state of confusion. I pulled out a pack of cigarettes but found it empty. I tossed it beneath one of the parked cars, cursing the day I became a police officer. I walked to a nearby grocery store and bought another pack.

The weather was gloomy and dust particles in the air limited visibility and diminished the sun's glare so a man felt he was suffocating inside a dirty bottle. Loudspeakers blared out the afternoon call to prayer, and the muezzin's voice was hoarse, doubling my soul's sorrow. Behind me, the middle-aged owner of the grocery was humbly repeating the muezzin's words.

I became aware of his existence as the resonance of his voice sent a quick spasm through my chest. I sat down on a filthy wooden chest and lit a cigarette. Looking up, I saw the apartment where Jasmine's family lived. Curiosity prompted the owner of the grocery to approach and ask me, 'Do you all know where she is?'

I shook my head: no. He gestured with his eyebrows toward the window directly opposite him and asked, 'Do you know that's her room?'

I turned toward him and almost smirked I was so delighted. In a tone devoid of emotion I asked, 'Are you sure?'

He replied confidently, 'Yes.'

I inquired as graciously as I could, 'Does she spend a lot of time at the window?'

Stroking his beard, he was slow to reply. 'I ask Almighty God's forgiveness ... what should I tell you, son? These are questions one shouldn't delve into.'

I felt even more strongly that he had something to tell me but felt awkward about stating plainly what was bubbling up inside him. Trying to wear down his resistance, I told him, 'Don't worry, Hajj – sorry, what is your esteemed name?

Swallowing, he replied, 'Sultan Atiq.'

I continued, 'Hajj Sultan, I'm a police inspector doing my duty. So you shouldn't feel awkward about providing me with some information. This is your legal obligation!'

He cleared his throat and began to play with his black prayer beads, 'The truth of the matter is that Hajj Nashir al-Ni'am's daughter's morals are so-so. She's reckless and likes to tease men.'

I nodded my head to encourage him to continue.

Half-closing one of his eyes he added, 'Even a grey-beard like me, who prays that God will provide him with a good ending to his life, was not spared her flirtations. She tried to tempt me, teasing me and my white hair at the end of my days.'

I moved closer and asked, 'What exactly did she do?'

He began to tense up and stuttered, 'I … I mean I would see her open the window and make rude gestures.'

Tightening the noose, I asked, 'Like what?'

Looking far away, toward Jasmine's window, he replied, 'I … I mean she bites into a cucumber while looking at me and winking. She licks ice cream and sticks her tongue out. She chews gum and makes bubbles that pop as if she's throwing me a kiss. Many times she has deliberately let her hair down at the window as if displaying it to me. Naughty things like this that girls do.'

When he had finished his statement, he released a sigh so deep it almost dislocated his ribs. I wondered whether it was conceivable that this senile grey-beard was vain enough to be in love with her. The way he sighed over her and the effort it had cost him to talk to me (in view of his admission) must show he was fond of her, consciously or not.

I reckoned that he loved Jasmine with every ounce of his being and that the fires of jealousy raging in his gut had prompted him to mention her to me. He seemed convinced that she had run away with a youth with whom she had fallen in love.

I couldn't let this golden opportunity slip away. So I asked, 'Hajj Sultan, I want you to tell me candidly: did you ever notice a young man from the neighbourhood who made repeated visits to your store and deliberately sat opposite her window to court her?'

He avoided my stern gaze, moistened his index finger and ran it down his neck. Then he raised his head to look up and whispered, 'Forgive me, Lord.' He gazed at her window and a fleeting gleam of jealousy sparked in his eyes. 'Yes,' he said, 'there was one.'

I snuffed out my cigarette and asked him nonchalantly, 'What's his name?'

He thrust his prayer beads into his coat pocket and busied himself with straightening his turban. 'His name is Ali Nashwan,' he said.

Taking the notebook from my pocket I recorded the name and then asked, 'Could you show me where he lives?'

He said, 'He's one of the building's residents, on the second floor. His apartment is right across from hers.'

I asked, 'How old is he?'

He replied, 'About eighteen.'

I asked, 'When was the last time you saw Jasmine?'

He answered, 'Yesterday at 7.30 in the morning; I saw her leave the building.'

I asked, 'Did you notice anything out of the ordinary about her? For example, did you notice whether she was carrying a suitcase or a large clothes bag?'

He said, 'No, she had a black handbag under her arm and a blue notebook with a hard cover, nothing else. But I noticed that the boy, whose name I just gave you, emerged immediately after her and followed her like a billy-goat.'

My heart pounded when I heard this valuable information and I asked, 'Are you sure it was Ali?'

He replied quickly, 'Yes it was. Every day he comes out right behind her and trails her like her own shadow.'

I recorded some quick observations in my notebook.

As he gave me a conspiratorial look he said, 'If you'll allow me, I'll close my shop. I want to catch the afternoon prayer at the mosque.'

I waited for him to shut up shop and then we said goodbye with a wave of the arm. He walked quickly toward a nearby mosque. I, for my part, put my trust in God and headed to Ali's apartment.

When I knocked on the door I heard a woman's voice ask from inside, 'Who is it?'

'Is Ali there?' I asked.

'Who wants him?' she asked.

'I'm his friend Abdurrabbih,' I replied.

In a minute, a solidly-built, tawny-complexioned man opened the door, his cheek swollen with *qat*. I guessed he was Ali's father and that he was between 47 and 50.

Narrowing his eyes he looked me up and down and said, 'Hello. Can I help you?'

Showing him my card, I told him, 'I'm Inspector Abdurrabbih al-Adini and I want to speak with Ali. Five minutes, no more.'

His eyes opened wide and he stepped back to allow me to enter. 'I'm his father. Come in. God has brought you.'

I didn't know whether to be encouraged or discouraged by his last statement. I heard footsteps hastening away and a muffled clamour. I realized that a large family was being corralled into a room at the far end of the apartment.

I entered a small, warm parlour and sat down. *Qat* twigs were strewn on the floor beside an ashtray filled with mangled cigarette butts, a third of which were stained with lipstick.

He sat down in the middle of the parlour and leaned back. He wanted to offer me a bundle of *qat* stems but I declined. He covered his feet with a wool blanket that would make him sweat, warm his body, and thus speed the arrival of the narcotic's euphoria.

Conscious that I was being observed through the keyhole of the closed door and that dozens of ears were listening, I asked, 'Where's Ali?'

He replied, 'Ever since Ali learned that the neighbours' daughter had left but not returned he's been searching the streets for her like a madman. Yesterday, he didn't come home till five in the morning. He had barely dozed for three hours when he went out to search for her. He hasn't had a bite to eat since yesterday and hasn't been to school. As you see it's 4 p.m. now and His Excellency hasn't returned. His mother has been weeping night and day and my heart hardly has the strength to beat I'm so worried about him.'

I commented sarcastically, 'Even her family hasn't searched for her this assiduously. Your son seems to be infatuated with her.'

'Sir, one proof of that is my son's discovery of Jasmine's bag and notebook.'

I was so surprised, thunderstruck, that I became tongue-tied.

He continued, 'I beg you, by the life of the person you hold most dear, keep this information to yourself and let it remain our secret. If the girl's family learn this, a calamity will ensue. They will eat my boy alive with their bare teeth and their daggers will shred his body before he has time to utter a word in his own defence.'

Approaching the case from a new angle, I said, 'I promise to keep the matter secret. Where are her effects?'

He said, 'Safe with my wife. Please wait a moment.'

He stood and cleared his throat loudly to warn his family to move away from the door.

Then he left, closing the door behind him. I heard a hushed debate, which was followed by weeping and sobbing. I inferred that Umm Ali was trying to prevent her husband from cooperating with me. Her fears for her son had doubtless caused her to distrust everyone.

Five grim minutes elapsed while I passed the time watching the wall clock. I shuddered when I saw the second hand flicker in one spot, unable to move forward. It was that rare moment when you see a functioning clock die before your eyes!

Finally Ali's father returned with a clothes bag, which he handed to me. Then he knelt before me. Out of an excess of caution, the bag's contents were in turn wrapped in three more bags. I found a woman's black handbag and a course notebook with a blue plastic cover. Opening the bag, I found Jasmine's university ID, some pens, a pencil, coins, a 1,000 riyal note and two fifties.

I also found a small address book, tissues, a chocolate bar, strawberry chewing gum, some bobby pins, jasmine perfume and dried blossoms, scraps of paper containing references and a lecture schedule. I flipped through the course notebook's three hundred pages quickly and observed that its owner had recorded her lessons systematically in an elegant hand. I put her effects back inside the three bags and asked Ali's father, whose brow was dripping with sweat, 'Where did your son find these?'

As he attempted to suppress a coughing fit that was racking his body he replied, 'He says he found them in the trees in the Faculty of Science garden.'

I pursed my lips and said, more to myself than to him, 'I must take him there so he can show me the precise location where he found the things.'

Sighing, as his eyes overflowed with tears, he said, 'If you went to the Faculty of Science now you might find him hanging out there, searching for more of her belongings.'

Rising, I said, 'Don't worry about your son. We'll keep an eye on him.'

I shook hands with him at the door of the apartment and thanked him for the valuable assistance he had provided the police. Many heads poked up behind him, perhaps ten. I left and descended the stairs, my head awash with doubts. Had he actually found these personal effects or was his family concealing the truth and trying to rid themselves of evidence against their son? I followed the back street to the main thoroughfare where my sergeant Muti' was waiting for me in a taxi. We shot off toward the Faculty of Science, which we reached in less than seven minutes.

We stopped near the faculty gate and I asked Sergeant Muti' to stay in the car and watch for a young man between seventeen and nineteen years of age. I got out of the vehicle and entered the faculty, heading toward the university's security office.

The duty officer saluted me and handed me a report half a page long. I read it but found no useful information. The guards hadn't noticed anything suspicious. They had searched the faculty's building four times without finding any clues. I laughed to myself at the stupidity of these blind soldiers who had failed to discover Jasmine's handbag and her course notebook, which a kid, who had the enthusiasm and dedication for the search, had found.

Folding the report and putting it in my pocket, I told the duty officer, 'We've found important items in the faculty garden that pertain to the missing girl.'

The duty officer's mouth fell open and his eyes bulged.

I continued threateningly, 'Consequently, you'll all have to answer for this lapse.'

As I left, I could hear the sound of the duty officer's feet hitting the floor with a thud. Zealously saluting me as I departed was his stupid attempt to apologize for failing to perform his duty. I went to the faculty garden, where the paths were almost deserted now that most of the students had gone home.

I was overwhelmed by the loud din made by the chirping sparrows and the nightingales, and by the cooing of the turtledoves. My eyes followed them as they flew gaily from tree to tree.

Feeling a pain in my chest, I turned toward a pomegranate tree about three metres away. I saw a white spectre move and then disappear into the trunk of the tree. My body trembled at this sight and I remained standing where I was, staring at the trunk, not knowing whether to doubt or believe the vision. Were my eyes at fault? Or was I overwrought because of this abominable case?

I wiped my face with my hand and felt relieved as this demonic notion faded away. I approached the fountain, which was turned off, and sat down to catch my breath. The garden was small, dominated by camphor trees and lofty white poplars. Scattered through the garden's reaches were arbours with facing seats that accommodated six. No one was around and except for the birds' love songs and the stirring music the wind wrested from the trees' boughs, calm enveloped the place.

I plunged my fingers into the fountain's still waters, which were covered with yellow leaves, and gazed at my reflection. My face undulated and lengthened each time a falling leaf struck the water's surface. I was amazed by the extent to which a flimsy yellow leaf could alter my features.

They say of a man whose time has come that his leaf has fallen. A small yellow leaf succumbs to the force of the wind and floats down. We are like that too: in a moment of despair we submit to death and give up the ghost.

I felt a spiritual presence in the garden and began to look around. Then I spotted a young man sitting in one of the arbours. His head was bowed and he was rigid: a lifeless statue. I won't deny that he spooked me a little. He seemed almost to have sprung from nowhere, becoming visible after being invisible.

I gained control of myself and walked toward him. I found myself involuntarily fingering my revolver and checking to see if it was in its holster at my waist. He heard my footsteps but didn't raise his head. He was staring at an invisible point somewhere beyond physical existence. His pupils were focused on the void, on a cavity not of this world. He was regarding something that has no name in our language, something we had never previously considered.

I cleared my throat and greeted him but he remained transfixed and oblivious. I sat down opposite him and asked gently, 'How are you, Ali?'

He raised his head and began to study my face, scrutinizing my features. I felt like fleeing his glance, which resembled damaging rays that penetrate deep beneath the skin.

Attempting to command his respect, I told him, 'I'm an inspector from Criminal Investigations and I've come to interrogate you.'

His eyes clouded and I sensed that his spirit's rays were fading and retreating. I continued in the gruff voice of an interrogator, 'Tell me, where did you discover Jasmine's handbag and course notebook?'

An unbearable minute of silence followed. His breathing quickened and his chest began to heave as if he were experiencing extreme difficulty getting enough air.

He stood up suddenly and walked off; I followed him, noticing for the first time that he was tall and plump, which made him look older than he was, even though he was still a boy, wet behind the ears, fifteen perhaps. Standing near the pomegranate tree he pointed to a cavity in its trunk.

I believed him right away.

I told myself: so that vision wasn't meaningless. An existential system governs matters like this; it's a system that remains beyond our ken.

Ali knelt and began to weep loudly while I was overcome by a terror I had never experienced before. I felt a holy presence and shook with fright when I heard the roar of water. The fountain had suddenly come back to life and begun to work; the water spilled out of its basin onto the ground on all sides.

I realized that my back was sweating, my ribs were trembling and my teeth were chattering. I felt ashamed of my weakness and failure of will. For the first time in my life I sensed that I was in the presence of a supernatural spiritual power, that my senses were on the blink and that my limbs were paralyzed.

I experienced a weird, incomprehensible state in which I was both inside my body and outside it at the same time, seeing it while it saw me, regarding it from every direction, as if I were a neutral external observer.

My intellect was crystal clear, free of emotion and feeling. The world around me twisted in spirals and spatial distances faded away as if I were experiencing an alternative form of existence.

The sun set and the shadows darkened gradually. Sergeant Muti', who had grown tired of waiting in the taxi, came to look for me. (I knew this because at this moment I was outside of my body, watching everything.) He spotted me standing in front of the pomegranate tree, sunk in a sublime state of contemplation.

He called to me from a distance but didn't dare approach. (Later he told me that he had felt an intense terror.)

I barely heard him. Then my worldly concerns returned. With sad, slow steps I withdrew from the garden, which was almost devoid of light, leaving behind me that boy and the pomegranate tree in a private reverie unspoiled by the presence of an interloper like me.

3
A Man Blinded to This Disconcerting World by Supernatural Delusions

My name is Nasir Salim al-Utmi and I'm the proprietor of the snack bar in the Faculty of Science; it's beside the wall and overlooks the garden.

I've earned my living in this location for twenty years. I'm as well versed about everything that happens in the administrative offices and the lecture halls as a judicious man is about his own home. I've got the lowdown on the professors and students – stuff their own families don't know. I'm the Faculty of Science's real archive!

As a result of my lengthy experience with the types of human beings who cause the floorboards of this scrap of earth to creak with their steps, I've learned to predict the fate of each person. This is an expertise gained from the experience of thousands of days and isn't knowledge that can be explained in books or taught to anyone else. A person wishing to emulate me would have to pursue my profession for twenty years.

All the same, the man has yet to be created who could boast that he can control his own fate or change it. Our destiny is manifest in our clothes, our conduct and our body language, which are the most obvious visible characteristics.

From my observation of simple things like these I can predict the unseen future, discern a trend and understand how a person strives to discover his fate. All science students who have chosen to wear bright yellow shirts, for example, have eventually ended up going crazy.

By selling sandwiches, juice and fries, I've been able to marry and buy a house for my family in the village. At the beginning of each Islamic month I send them their living expenses. I've been granted ten kids: four boys and six girls. I've educated all of them till they finished the junior high school diploma. I've definitely not encouraged them to complete their education and have plucked from their minds any notion whatsoever of attending the university.

What I've observed in the university bears no relation to real knowledge. Behind the glittering academic façade, what students reap is shit. Do you know what our university's greatest achievement is? It's turning the human being who registers here into a donkey!

This work isn't easy; not even the expert sleight-of-hand of the conjurers in our rural areas can turn such a huge number of human beings into asses. In my village there's a weekly market on Tuesday (al-Thuluth) where normally no more than five to ten donkeys are sold. Here, however, we have a far larger market for donkeys and the cool thing is that each donkey carries an ID so they won't confuse him with the other asses! That's not necessary in our village market because each donkey there is easily distinguishable from the others.

The professor in our university gulls the students and gives them summary lectures that are more like magician's tricks. Then the students cheat the professor, using his own methods, and pass.

No genuine scholar or inventor has ever graduated from here. Even if one of them tried to accomplish something, the numbskull majority would be propelled by ruinous envy to drop him from their group and to destroy him psychologically and physically. Anyone who displays any genius here is digging his own grave. His gifts will turn everyone around him into loaded revolvers pointed at his chest.

My kids are really bright and that's why I've forbidden them to pursue a higher education, because I fear the anger and vengeance of slackers against them. I'm not joking or exaggerating.

With my own eyes, over the course of twenty years I've seen dozens of born geniuses destroyed and devastated by fiendish spite. Moral depravity is so endemic here that a man can almost smell it in the air! Prostitution rings scout the female students, harvesting an abundant crop, and brokers for 'touristic marriage' offer their services in broad daylight.

What's amazing is the way a male student gazes at a female classmate. It's an inappropriate stare devoid of respect. He relates to her not as a fellow student of science but as a student of copulation!

Most of the professors are cultured and ethical but even in the teaching corps there are some rotten apples. Last year, Dr. Aqlan was the perpetrator of a moral scandal that ended in a grievous tragedy. We had a student here, Waddah, who was exceptionally bright. Of his peers he was the only one who did well in almost all his subjects. But even though he was extremely smart he wasn't able to retain the top place because he failed one course, the one taught by Dr. Aqlan.

Do you know why? Because he was too good looking!

The girls flocked around him and competed for his attention because his appearance transformed him into a legend in their eyes. They could talk about nothing else.

My snack bar has a section reserved for girls. It's screened from sight by curtains so students who wear a face veil can remove their *niqab* and eat in comfort. I'm the only man who has the right to go in and out of their nest, see their faces and hear their chatter. They take my presence for granted and drop their guard, perhaps because I seem as old as their fathers.

This privileged position has provided me with an inside knowledge of what happens in the closeted world of girls, allowing me to gauge how fond they were of Waddah. I even heard one of them say brazenly that Waddah was the only man in the faculty to rouse her passion and that when she saw him, she felt a tremor in her vagina and a quivering of her labia. Out of the corner of my eye I watched her demonstrate to her classmates how her labia had trembled. She stuck her hand out horizontally and then placed her thumb over the four other fingers, which she had clenched, thus creating a model. Then she waggled her thumb against the other fingers lightly and swiftly for two minutes.

We all used to tell ourselves – us guys – how lucky he was. But his luck ended when Dr. Aqlan's eyes spotted him. Then his good looks became a curse. The poor boy tried various means to revise his examination paper, but Dr. Aqlan had only one request for him and threatened to fail him in every subject he taught if Waddah didn't comply with this demand.

Dr. Aqlan's family lives in the countryside and he lives alone in the apartment the university provides for him. Dr. Aqlan entices his victims – male and female – to this empty apartment, where he takes sexual liberties with them.

To that depraved apartment Waddah slunk and yielded to his professor's pressure. Only a few days afterwards, Dr. Aqlan posted a form on the division's bulletin board to announce a change in Waddah's grade. He gave him 100 per cent for the subject!

This announcement created a scandal that destroyed Waddah's reputation; it constituted a blemish to his character and offered conclusive evidence for anyone who wished to condemn Waddah's conduct. All the students – male and female – knew that Waddah had compromised his pride and slept in the same bed as this homosexual.

It was the talk of the faculty. Even the janitors – male and female – talked trash about Waddah, mocked him and sang songs about him with altered lyrics. His male classmates, who already hated him secretly because of the girls' infatuation with him, condemned him and spoke contemptuously about him, alluding to this deviant relationship.

His life became a hell and he lost his self-confidence, which had once been high, till he could no longer look anyone in the eye. He fell apart and was slaughtered by our eyes when we gazed at him coldly and vindictively as if he were a cockroach surrounded by a battalion of shoes ready to crush him.

He couldn't take it. I happened to hear a conversation between some friends, one of whom shared Waddah's room. He said some rude, disgusting stuff, claiming that Waddah had fungal infections on the upper portions of his ears and that on the inside repulsive growths showed that his skin was putrescent. He claimed that Dr. Aqlan's saliva was to blame. He had allegedly placed Waddah's ear in his mouth, licking it with his tongue. Then he had nipped the ear and greedily sucked blood from it. This may have been a slanderous comment and false. When a scandal erupts, people love to share figments of their imagination, like guests at a banquet. On this occasion, the banquet was Waddah's body, that angelic form they had long envied.

Waddah wasn't seen at the faculty for a week and then we heard he had killed himself.

This year, Dr. Aqlan has repeated his offence but this time the victim was a female, a beautiful student named Jasmine Nashir al-Ni'am. He failed her, even though he knew her grades in the rest of her subjects ranged from very good to excellent.

When she went to consult him, he suggested dealing with the matter in his normal way. I heard her ask her girlfriends, while she ate a liver sandwich, the meaning of 'marjoram'. None of them knew. My response was to turn my back and listen even more intently.

She explained to the other girls, 'Dr. Aqlan promised he would pass me in his subject if I let him press the marjoram.'

The girls stopped swallowing their food and lowered their heads. They had caught on, but no one said a word.

Five years ago, Dr. Aqlan moved his office to the third floor, making a point of choosing a room that had a window overlooking my snack bar and the garden. Since this window is located on the side nearest the wall, it is considered by far the best observatory for spying on the female students who frequent the girls' wing of my snack bar.

From that ill-omened window Dr. Aqlan could see Jasmine's face and contemplate her charms as if sipping from an extraordinarily sweet and delicious cup of honey.

Jasmine is brown and as slender as a stalk of sugar cane. She's so feminine that she slays hearts even when fully veiled. Her eyes are wide and her black pupils glow with tenderness and sweetness. The impact of her eyelashes, which are thick and long, is almost magical. If she glances at a man he's struck by a sickness he can't shake off; passion for her will flow through his veins, mixed with his blood, till Judgement Day. The more access to her and the more contact with her he has achieved, the more likely it is that he'll sink into insanity and die.

I swear to God that my eyes have never seen a girl this beautiful at any time since I arrived in the faculty twenty years ago. No girl comparable to her in beauty will ever turn up here, not even in another twenty years.

I believe that God grants us one Queen Bilqis every thousand years. At the beginning of each millennium He sends us as a magnificent gift one Queen of Sheba like Bilqis: a peerless, legendary beauty. This precious gift comes only once every millennium. That's how it is with presents from the King of Kings!

Like a hovering owl, this question has haunted the heads of everyone entering or leaving the faculty: will Jasmine yield and surrender her virginity to Dr. Aqlan or will she resist?

Male and female students and staff can find no other topic to discuss. Most think she will fall. The girls closest to her, the women who know her best, affirm that she will never bargain away her honour. If push comes to shove she'll drop her university studies and stay home.

I think that Jasmine's female classmates are probably right. After gazing at her features I have determined that she has a forceful personality, a strong will and a proud, defiant spirit that radiates self-assurance and self-reliance. That's why I think that Dr. Aqlan has made a huge mistake; no matter how much power and authority he has, he will never succeed in subduing her. Jasmine won't deliver her body to him, even if this refusal causes her death.

A mean-spirited rumour has been flying through the faculty to the effect that Jasmine, whose family have declared her missing, has spent the week in Dr. Aqlan's apartment. May God curse them for accusing her of licentiousness at a time when no one knows whether the girl is dead or alive.

The police have been investigating Dr. Aqlan and his apartment. The suspicions they nourish about him are supported by powerful corroborating evidence. They think Jasmine visited him in his apartment to sort out her problem with him and that she resisted his attempts to flirt with her. Then he raped her. Fearful that men of her tribe would seek revenge, he killed her and hid her body.

A police inspector, whose name I don't recall, visited me yesterday. He's brown-skinned, tall and clean-shaven but with a moustache. His hair is curly like an African's, but his nose is as sharp as a dagger and his teeth are yellow from smoking.

He appeared here half an hour before sunset when I had finished cleaning and tidying up and was preparing to leave.

He told me, 'We're looking for a student named Jasmine who's been missing for a week. Do you know her?'

I took a chance and mumbled, 'Yes.'

He flicked his cigarette pack at the bottom and a cigarette shot into the air like a flying fish. He caught it and lit it with a cheap, red lighter. I was astounded by his dexterity and accuracy. How could he extract just one cigarette with only a light tap?

Blowing smoke toward the ceiling he asked, 'When did you last see her?'

I replied, 'On Valentine's Day, when she entered the girls' wing she called me and handed me a sprig of basil. So I thanked her and placed the sprig behind my ear. Her impulsive gesture made me blush with embarrassment and disconcerted me, even though, to be frank, I'm not at all bashful around women. But Jasmine is a special case; she would inspire emotions even in a stone. She ordered a liver sandwich, hot, and chilled pomegranate juice. She sat in that corner, facing the sunlight, and her girlfriends swarmed around her. They began to ask if she had received a present from a boyfriend or even a lover. She told them she hadn't met the love of her life yet and opened her black handbag to show them its contents. She may have wanted to silence malicious tongues and to declare before the largest possible group of witnesses that she hadn't received a Valentine's Day present from Dr. Aqlan.

'I heard the male students say that at the end of his lecture that Dr. Aqlan had asked Jasmine to stay after class. No one knew what they discussed but they were alone for fifteen minutes. The students believed that he had given her an expensive present for Valentine's Day. The malicious ones laughed sarcastically, claiming that Dr. Aqlan had been guided by God to shun depravity and to seek a heterosexual relationship.

'Jasmine didn't finish her liver sandwich but merely nibbled a small portion of it. She drank the pomegranate juice slowly, as if it were bitter medicine. Her friends went off to the next lecture but she stayed behind, alone. She would turn the glass around in her hand and take small sips, which she savoured in her mouth for a time before swallowing. She was lost in deep reflection and an indescribable sorrow clouded her face.

'My heart was consumed by pain for her, but what could someone like me do? I had a daydream that I had an automatic rifle with which I was threatening Dr. Aqlan. I forced him to give Jasmine the grades she deserved, but this was a hollow type of heroism that ended with a lengthy sigh.

'It was almost 11 a.m. when Jasmine stood up heavily and paid her tab. Then I saw her head out to the garden. She chose the seat beside the pomegranate tree. I'm not sure why, but I was overcome then by a powerful feeling that she was weeping.

'A sandstorm blew in and the dust made it impossible to see. Some umbrellas fell to the ground so I left my kitchen to set them back up. It took me five minutes to complete this task. When I returned and glanced at Jasmine I was flabbergasted to find a man, whose back was toward me, seated across from her.

'Although I was busy with many chores I attempted as best I could to keep an eye on her. I'll tell you frankly I had reservations about that man. Worried and anxious, I confused some of my orders because I felt so stressed and distracted. A dispute broke out between me and an unruly student. It would have ended in fisticuffs had good people not intervened. During this minute, when my eyes were off her, Jasmine departed. From that moment I've never seen her again. When I gestured to the man she had been with to ask where she had gone, he opened a white book and pointed to its pages. I ignored him and paid him no heed. I was busy taking orders and don't know when he left the garden.'

The officer jotted some quick notes in his little book and then asked me, making a fresh start, 'Describe that man for me.'

Scratching my head I told him, 'I wasn't able to see his face. I saw the back of his head. He was middle-aged and powerfully built. His shoulders were wide and his white hair, which was sleek, glittered like diamonds in the sunshine. As I recall this image now, it occurs to me that his hair colour was unique. Its whiteness glistened so powerfully that it dazzled me!'

Looking at me sceptically, as if doubting the accuracy of my description, he asked, 'What was he wearing?'

I said, 'I don't recall.'

He knitted his brows and said, 'Try to remember.'

I looked down for a moment, trying to recollect. Oddly, I hadn't noticed his clothes, neither their cut nor their colour. The one thing that was fixed in my memory was the whiteness of his hair and how it shone like a precious gem.

The setting sun left a dreary gloom in its wake. I lit a yellow candle and started to make tea.

Watching me intently he asked, 'Do you believe there is any relationship between that man and Jasmine's disappearance?'

'I don't know.'

'Do you know who he is?'

'No.'

'Does he resemble anyone?'

I turned toward him, handed him a steaming glass of tea, and answered, 'He resembles no one else I know. I told you, sir, his distinctive characteristic, which will allow you to identify him, is his white hair.'

He grimaced as if suffering from acid reflux and then asked me, 'Are you married?'

'Yes, and I have ten children.'

'Where do you all live?'

'I live nearby in a room that doesn't even have a bath and my family lives in the village, in a house we own.'

He brought his face close to mine and asked, 'Why don't they live with you?'

Shrugging, I responded, 'My finances don't allow me to rent an apartment in the city for my family.'

He stared into my eyes for so long that a shudder of alarm racked my intestines. He turned and left without a word of farewell.

His fierce, accusatory look frightened me; I was shaking when I closed the snack bar. I began to imagine myself in a dungeon where interrogators took turns goading me with slaps, kicks and taunts. Under pressure from their torture I confessed I was responsible for Jasmine's demise.

I didn't go anywhere but headed straight to my room. When I stuck out my hand in the dark I noticed that the flange for the padlock's latch had been moved. Someone had taken it off together with the lock and reinstalled it slightly lower down the door. I undid the padlock, lit the lamp and immediately realized that the police had searched my room while I was away.

I quickly pulled the milk powder can from beneath the bed and opened it. My money was all there, untouched, but a chill penetrated my heart.

It was my fault. I had told many people about the stranger who had been with Jasmine during that last hour before her disappearance. Some of them had obviously been informants who squealed on me to the police, relaying my words to them. This had led them to train their sights on me. I don't know what they suspect me of? I don't believe they could possibly nourish any doubts about me. Oh, if only I had cut out my tongue before I blurted out a single word! They'll drag me involuntarily into this case's labyrinth. When they see fit, they'll lean on me and interrogate me with a lot of Q-and-A until the case is concluded – assuming it ever is.

I despise this blighted university, which is teeming with informants who hide like lizards in cracks and crevices. For twenty years I've dealt cautiously with them. Now, like a callow youth, I've tumbled into the cesspool of their gossip. If I emerge safely from this case, surviving the beatings, imprisonment and humiliation it brings me, I promise God I'll slaughter a ram and distribute the meat as alms to the poor and needy.

4
The Sacrificial Lamb

My name is Ali Nashwan. I am just four-and-a-half years short of twenty.

Four years ago we moved into the building where Jasmine lives. Fortunately for me, the doors of our apartments face each other.

That first year she was allowed to play with me. We played school. She was the teacher and I was the student. She taught me amazing things about ancient Yemeni civilizations, about Ma'in, Saba'[1] and Himyar. One of our lessons still sticks in my mind with all its details. It concerned the engineering behind the construction of the Ma'rib Dam in the Sabaean age. Whenever I remember this lesson I'm amazed at her ability to comprehend difficult matters like these. How could she have reached an understanding of such complex questions when, at the time, she was only sixteen? I was awed by the depth and breadth of her knowledge and began to consider her the equivalent of inventors and geniuses like Alexander Graham Bell and Marconi.

We also played doctor. She was the physician and I was the patient. I recall that she implanted forty kidneys and seven hearts in my chest!

When we played palace, she was the princess and I was the jinni. We fought each other with wooden swords and cardboard armour. She always won. When I protested against this uniform

---

1 Sheba

result she explained her philosophy of life: 'Good must always vanquish evil.'

On my return from school my mind would be full of her. I would eat lunch and then study my lessons throughout the siesta. When her father left their apartment for the afternoon prayer I would pick up my maths book and knock on her door. She was usually the one who opened the door and her smile was sweeter than cream.

Before entering I would ask if she wanted anything from the grocery store. Winking playfully, she would remove the coins hidden in her bra and send me to the grocer's to buy her favourite kind of cookie. I would clasp the coins in my fist, feeling their heat and wishing I were one of those lucky coins!

I would descend the stairs while she closed the door. On the landing I would open my fist and enjoy kissing the coins and smelling the fragrance they had acquired from touching her splendid body. I would be panting by the time I reached Hajj Sultan's shop, where I would point to a triangular cookie dipped in chocolate. He would take the money and hand me my order while twisting his moustache with his other hand.

By the way, Jasmine is a first-rate gourmet and when a new type of cookie reaches the market she will be one of the first to buy it. She can render a verdict on its quality after one bite. If she shouts with joy and delight that means the cookie has met with her approval. Then she will tell everyone she meets about this new cookie, advising each person to purchase it. If she wrinkles her brow and purses her lips that means she doesn't like it. Then she'll throw the rest in the trash.

I would return, leaping up three steps at a time. Even before I rang the bell I would find that Jasmine had opened the door and was hiding behind it. I would pretend I didn't see her and didn't know what she had in mind. She would stick out a leg to trip me and I would fall to the floor, which was covered by blue carpeting. I would scatter the cookies everywhere, and we would compete with each other to pick them up. In this silly way we divided the cookies between us, each reaping a share commensurate with our cleverness and speed.

We would sit in the living room, where she would go over my difficult maths lessons with me. She took extraordinary pains to help me understand but I would be in a daze, unable to grasp anything. All the time that she was busy explaining and simplifying equations, I would be gazing avidly at her face, devouring her features, never satiated. The more I looked at her the hungrier and more filled with longing I grew.

What bewildering secret in her face so enchanted me that I couldn't take my eyes off her, not even for a second? The strange thing was that I was completely incapable of retaining her image in my mind. I was totally unable to sketch her features in my imagination. I could study her for hours and hours a day, but when I was alone I would fail to recall her face, as if she were a creature that existed only in fables.

When I forced my imagination to produce a picture of her I saw emanations of unknown origin sully her image and distort her head. The beloved and familiar form morphed into a terrifying creature, a savage beast from which worms and venomous vermin crawled.

Whenever I tried to concentrate and to construct her beloved body with my intellect, I saw disturbing colours run over her eyes and mouth. Every attempt I made to exert my will ended in bitter disappointment.

The really weird thing was that when I closed my eyes and tried to call to mind the image of any creature other than her, I recalled it without any difficulty worth mentioning. When I thought, for example, of Hajj Sultan, the proprietor of the grocery store, his picture was readily created in my mind, despite the fact that I had never made any effort, great or small, to recall him.

Inside me there is another will I don't control; it attempts to expel Jasmine from my imagination. This shadowy spectre hates and disfigures Jasmine. I struggle against an unknown force inside me. I build my love for Jasmine stone by stone, but it destroys this love and pulls up its foundations. I lift my beloved to the ranks of the angels, but this other spirit that inhabits me reduces her to base images, at times a mouse, at other times a spider!

When the lesson ended, I would try to keep her with me for as long as I could by asking her about topics more mature than my years. I wanted passionately to hold her attention as well as to show her that I was an intelligent youth. I used to ask her questions about anything that crossed my mind, questions that ran the gamut from politics, economics and scientific achievements to God, miracles, the jinn and cheating in exams.

Jasmine was like a wise teacher for me, and thanks to her I refrained from cheating and writing cheat sheets and began to treat people according to a high-minded ethic. My interests expanded in an unprecedented way and I grew excited about reading children's magazines and stories from around the world. I loved collecting stamps and coins and became interested in my diet, in brushing my teeth and in doing fitness exercises. Over and above all this, I found the gumption to buy a tambourine with brass castanets, which I played when my father wasn't home.

There were some videogames in her house but she didn't like playing them. She claimed they hurt your eyes and that people hooked on them started to wear glasses prematurely.

Jasmine taught me how to play chess, but I'm not fond of this complicated game, which reveals my dreadful ignorance. So I avoided lingering at her place after she had removed that heavy wooden box from her armoire. I used to claim I had a stomach-ache and leave, holding my belly, followed by her sceptical gaze. When Her Majesty noticed a correlation between my bouts of diarrhoea and the appearance of that hateful box, out of pity for me and my tummy she stopped bringing it out.

She asked me once what I wanted to be when I grew up. I told her I wanted to be a government minister. Laughing, she asked, 'Do you want to become a government minister so bodyguards will march before and behind you down the street?'

Feeling hurt by her laughter I told her, 'No, I'm not a scaredy-cat. I'll carry a revolver tucked into my belt when I walk. I want to be a government minister so I can have a palace with a garden and a jerry-can special[2] and…' The words were on the tip of my tongue but froze there and I didn't complete the sentence.

'And what else?' she demanded.

Flushed with embarrassment I stammered and said in a low voice, 'And I'll marry you.'

Her eyes opened wide and she laughed so hard her chest hurt. Then she seized my hand and dragged me to her mother to tell her I intended to marry her.

At that moment I felt a terrifying dizziness, my eyes were blinded, my mouth felt dry, my knees shook and I wanted the earth to open up and swallow me. To my surprise, Jasmine's mother didn't get angry and didn't think of beating me. Instead, she burst into resounding laughter and her fingers began to tousle my hair.

On another occasion, I asked Jasmine about her ambitions for the future. Then she replied that she wanted to become an archaeologist and that excavating the ruins of ancient Yemeni civilizations and studying them was the dream of her life.

She told me about the ancient Yemenis, who took the moon for a God named Almaqah and built huge temples to honour him. They offered sacrifices to him and launched wars in his name. They believed that the secret to their great wealth lay in obedience to his word. Jasmine herself was very fond of the moon and waited for it to appear every night. That made

2 A Toyota Land Cruiser

me wonder whether she secretly worshipped it. Naturally this was a silly idea, because worship of the pagan god Almaqah died out in ancient times and no one on the face of the earth still embraces it.

Later, when she felt more self-confident, she repeatedly visited the National Museum where treasures of ancient Yemen are stored. I would play along with her interest in these remains of the past out of love for her, not for ancient civilizations. As a matter of fact, I didn't think they were worth much. I was incredulous that people spent so lavishly to preserve these artifacts.

She had scientific encyclopaedias with coloured bindings and a lot of books about ancient ruins. She consulted these repeatedly without ever growing tired of them. Occasionally she would vary her reading habits and pick up a detective story by Agatha Christie or a book of poems by Nizar Qabbani.

I would dawdle in their home till it was time for supper and then everyone would insist that I stay and eat with them. So I would, feeling slightly uncomfortable. But the warmth of their glances and the goodness of their hearts dissolved the psychological barrier between us and left me feeling part of the family.

Jasmine's mother's food is unparalleled and has a wonderful aroma. Anyone who has tasted it once will never forget it as long as he lives. I found myself captivated by the dishes Jasmine's mother prepared and by their wonderful taste, so I started inventing excuses to linger in their apartment till suppertime arrived.

This arrangement lasted for a full year, but a despicable slander from Hajj Sultan the grocer turned Jasmine's life upside down and ended the most beautiful chapter in my life. One day he waited for Jasmine's father to return in the evening and then told him his daughter had played ball in the street with other girls, exposing her legs, and that the neighbourhood's young men ('the Rogues') had formed a circle around the girls and showered them with shameless expressions of love.

When Jasmine's father got home her mother had the supper set out as usual. She and Jasmine were sitting on one side and I on the other, leaving the place of honour for the paterfamilias, whom we had been awaiting. Jasmine's three older brothers are all serving in the armed forces.

When Nashir al-Ni'am stormed out of the bathroom, slamming the door behind him with all his might, my heart fell. I felt that an inescapable calamity was descending on us. He took his vacant place, his face pulsing with anger. His eyes glittering, he asked Jasmine, 'Is it true that you played ball in the street?'

Jasmine looked down, intimidated by the look in his eyes, and replied in a feeble voice, 'Yes.'

He screamed at her, 'Didn't I forbid you to play in the street?'

Jasmine's face turned white and her eyes welled-up.

Roaring like a raging camel he continued, 'Nincompoop, why did you disobey my command?'

He picked up the dishes from the table and began to pour food over Jasmine's head. She burst into tears but didn't budge. Blinded by rage Nashir al-Ni'am rose and then fell upon her like a savage beast, kicking and slapping her. Jasmine was moaning and weeping but didn't resist him. Her mother was wailing and screaming but fear prevented her from intervening. As for me, I was appalled by the horror of the situation and almost wet myself. I slipped away without anyone noticing and fled home.

Whenever I remember my cowardly, weak-kneed reaction I feel ashamed and disgraced. I blame myself for not trying to defend Jasmine and protect her from her father's brutality. I could at least have shoved my body between them, even if I would have been beaten.

The chance of a lifetime to show her my gallantry had arrived but I had reacted in such a pathetic way that I lost her respect and sank in her opinion. In her hour of need I had deserted her. I fled to save my skin and abandoned her as if I didn't know her!

I admit that this horrible situation is my single worst memory, the black spot on my record and a curse. I am prepared to sacrifice half my life to erase this ill-fated incident from my karma. If only it had never happened! If only it had happened to someone else!

This incident was a turning point in Jasmine's life; overnight she moved from the world of children to the world of women. She began to veil her face whenever she left her apartment and they secluded her from contact with males. They even prevented me from visiting her.

Jasmine was suddenly out of reach; approaching her had become impossible. Separation from her was a knockout blow for me. It was as if I had lost both my parents at once, as if this beautiful world had spat me out. For a time I held a grudge against Hajj Sultan because he seemed a cunning devil who had conspired against me, expelling me from my paradise.

I was so sad I became depressed. I spoke little, didn't move around much and didn't feel like playing. I spent hours staring into space. From time to time I would sigh bitterly and this troubled my mother, who told me that only a debtor or a miscreant who feared being hurled into the dark recesses of prison would moan like this. I would reply that I was concerned about my studies and feared I would fail this year.

She was so worried about me that she rolled her eyes, and her love squirrelled away a grief like mine inside her. She kept me company in my torment – even though she was preoccupied by caring for my younger brothers – and suffered along with me as if she were part of my body.

I didn't even feel like eating and lost half my weight. My bones stuck out and my clothes were too big for me. My loss of weight in this sudden manner made my father suspect I had contracted a serious illness. So he made the rounds of the hospitals with me and many tests were performed on me. He was eventually convinced, although with difficulty, that I was healthy and not suffering from any malady, even if he would occasionally declare that modern doctors knew nothing about medicine.

Six months later, a thought occurred to me that seemed eminently sensible. It was that by eating a lot I would grow up fast and consequently could, at the earliest opportunity, present myself to Jasmine's family as a suitor for her hand. These hopes, which sprouted within me, brought back my appetite and I wolfed down copious quantities of food. So my weight increased and I grew taller. By exerting an enormous amount of willpower to force my body to yield to the idea that governed me I succeeded. Today I possess a powerful body and look like a tall, broad-shouldered man.

All ties between the two of us were severed and we didn't even exchange greetings, as if our shared memories were an odious crime that should be renounced and atoned for. It seemed that for Jasmine to wear a *niqab*, to cover her face with a piece of black cloth, was a sign that she had lost her memory and a warning that she had voluntarily broken with the past and forgotten it.

The *niqab* was a black banner a girl in the neighbourhood flew to announce a rupture with boys her age, a statement that even if she had known them in the past she didn't know them now. She had declared war on their previous friendship. Thanks to the *niqab*, Jasmine, the friend and confidante whom I had seen almost every day, became a stranger, a creature from another world.

In my dreams back then I saw myself crashing against strands of barbed wire, which multiplied and grew like jungle trees as I tried to cross endless black walls. Even though Jasmine had renounced the past and pretended not to know me, I, quite unlike her, became ever more attached to her and my infatuation grew.

Her presence enveloped me as if I were a foetus in her womb. Every breath that escaped my lungs whispered her name. Each of my gestures was deliberate, as if I lived under her constant supervision.

I rearranged my armoire and used only part of my bed, as if she were living with me in the same room. I would tell myself this would appeal to her taste and that would not. I wasted a lot of time in internal debates about what she would and would not like.

I had resolved to marry her and to bring her back to this humble playpen of mine. So every day I made a huge effort to keep the room clean and tidy, to beautify and decorate it.

I imagined her combing her hair before my mirror, pulling out a drawer to get her lipstick, napping on my bed and pulling the coverlet that we shared over to her side as she enjoyed sweet dreams.

My sudden and compulsory separation from Jasmine caused an eruption of my dormant sexual volcanoes. Lusty fantasies totally overwhelmed me. My flaccid, boyish prick began to torment me, becoming erect when I walked on the street and saw girls my age. I would feel quite uncomfortable, believing that all the passers-by noticed my distended member. That thought caused me unbearable psychological torment. I tried to goad my brain into issuing stern orders to that rebellious organ to cease its display, but it ignored my brain's orders and stubbornly persisted in its swelling erection!

Now I can laugh at myself for blushing, turning pale, feeling anxious and walking awkwardly when I thought people spotted it, even though it was concealed by my clothes and no one noticed it. These were immature fantasies, a child's embarrassment at the onset of puberty.

In my jurisprudence class, the teacher gave lectures about major ritual impurity and menstruation, the difference between semen and pre-seminal fluid, which of them makes full ritual cleansing obligatory as opposed to partial ablution, and other topics that concerned the genitalia of men and women. Then I would feel my blood boil with lust and my brain overheat and flare up while my little friend grew long and hard.

I would suffer in agony and want to flee from the class for fear of becoming fully aroused and climaxing so that the white fluid the professor had given us a headache by discussing would flow over the classroom's floor tiles as I ejaculated, publicly humiliating me so I became the butt of jokes by the students and teachers. They might even expel me from school on account of my disgraceful deed.

I was frightened by these erections that I couldn't control and was apprehensive about the untoward consequences of the scourge of having an orgasm at an inappropriate moment – in class, for example – when I would be scolded and beaten for my lack of manners. I would wonder whether I would suffer my whole life from my little friend's erections.

I would grieve and tell myself that perhaps I wasn't like other boys. After I dreamt of Jasmine, I was afflicted by enormous regret that I had awakened before consummating my lovemaking with her. Then I would blame myself and decide that in my next dream I wouldn't open my eyes and would continue my dream to its culmination.

When I turned thirteen and reached puberty I became a devoted practitioner of masturbation, jerking off at least once a day and occasionally two or three times in a single day. My daily routine didn't change. When I returned home from school I would eat lunch and apply myself to my lessons. After finishing my homework I would relieve my tension by ejaculating a large quantity of fluid. By then it would be time for the afternoon prayer and I would descend to the street, where I would buy a bottle of cola from Hajj Sultan and three triangular cookies dipped in chocolate. I would sit outside on the store's bench where I would eat and drink deliberately until the sun set. All the while my eyes were trained cautiously and slyly on Jasmine's window.

Jasmine would occasionally peek out from her window, but there might be lean days when she didn't appear at all. Hajj Sultan was annoyed that I sat for hours on the bench outside his store and made rude comments to make me leave, but I endured his malice and impudent remarks for Jasmine's sake. Any day that my eye was graced by the light of her face I felt joy and contentment. Then I would depart, feeling thankful for her kindness, as bliss settled deep inside me.

On a day when I was denied her presence and the sight of her I would feel low for the rest of the evening and peace of mind would find no way to my door. Apprehensions and suspicions would afflict me and I would say perhaps something has happened to her. Perhaps she's too ill to stand and grant our street a momentary glance of greeting. Perhaps her boorish father has learned that I wait every afternoon to delight my eyes with a glimpse of her lethal beauty and has forbidden her to approach the window.

If her beloved head did not peek out, night would descend on me while I was stationed in my spot. I would be still hoping she would appear and disperse the gloom, but she never appeared at her window after dark. On ill-omened days I would be on the verge of tears when I returned home, feeling a grief larger than the oceans. My mood would be turbulent and mercurial. When I sat down to supper with my family the least word could set me off. I would become nervous, rash, querulous and prone to express my annoyance by yelling and kicking pieces of furniture.

When I retired to bed a crazy desire to slip into Jasmine's apartment would tempt me. I could scale the external drainpipes and gain entry through a bathroom or kitchen window that had been left open. I could invade her bedroom to kneel by her bed while she slept. Then I could quench my thirst by gazing at her fascinating face.

I assumed I could continue contemplating her face to my heart's content with no objection from her to cause me any anxiety. I would be oblivious to any creature besides her. Then I could absorb her features at leisure, hour after hour, until the cock crowed to announce that dawn was dancing on the distant horizon.

I was happy when there was some disturbance on our street, a quarrel between two women who were neighbours or a fight between two boys, because when the shouting grew loud and people gathered, curiosity would induce my beloved to poke her head out of the window so she could observe what was going on. I secretly prayed that God would multiply the disputes on our street and fill it with disturbances!

When Jasmine entered the university our routes coincided. Then I would press myself against the inside of our apartment door and watch through its peephole for her to emerge. When she opened her door she would glance at the glass peephole and then quickly descend the stairs. Once I could no longer hear her footsteps I would open my door and pursue her.

While I walked behind her I would forget the world around me, thinking only of her. I would savour her charms the way a coffee connoisseur sips one drop at a time. Although only a few metres separated me from her, my mind would try to eliminate it. I imagined myself cleaving to her, pressing my body against her hot, tempting flesh.

I would stockpile in my memory images of all her curves and the sway of her tantalizing body so I could recall them when I was alone and use them in a shameless imaginary love tryst in which each of us would offer our body to the other liberally and generously.

I would focus all my senses and my spirit on her dancing buttocks, which resembled the two palms of a drummer beating a drum of delights. I was so filled with desire that I could have ignited.

I observed her rump so often that I began to walk like her, taking feminine, fluid steps as my buttocks rose and fell, even though this has created some problems for me. I began my day with divine enjoyment of these beauties and a lecherous pursuit that gave me a feeling of intoxication and unruly vigour.

On February 14th I awoke feeling blue and got up recalling the remnants of a vile dream. I entered the bathroom and attended to my needs. Then I took my father's razor and began to stroke the hairless skin above my mouth. They say this is a way to encourage your moustache to sprout faster and to make the individual hairs plentiful and long, like the Turks' moustaches.

My hand trembled foolishly and I cut myself, making my face bleed. I washed my face with soap and water and left the bathroom with my finger on the wound to prevent any further bleeding.

I put on my boring school uniform – it's a dusty sand colour – and turned the shirt collar up. I sprinkled cologne on my chest and combed my hair while scrutinizing my attire in front of the mirror. My mother called me from the kitchen. I picked up my books, which were wrapped in a prayer rug, and checked the clock, which indicated that it was 7.25 a.m.

I reflected that Jasmine would leave her apartment shortly and rushed to the kitchen. Standing, I ate large helpings of the red beans that my mother excels at cooking and drank a glass of milk so hot it burned my tongue. I washed off in the kitchen sink despite my mother's protests and, waving goodbye to her and my young brothers, ran toward the door of our apartment. I picked up the brush and a shoe, which I began to polish, standing up while looking through the peephole.

My mother suddenly emerged from the kitchen and I squatted down and busied myself with the shoe. She cast me a concerned look and entered the bathroom. So I stood up again and began to watch the door of Jasmine's apartment through the peephole. My tiresome younger brothers rushed out of the kitchen too and began to jump and punch each other all around me, but I ignored them.

Despite the mayhem surrounding me I heard the rattling of the door facing us. Then I heard the creaking of the door's hinges and saw Jasmine emerge from her apartment, walking haughtily and holding her head high like a queen.

With extraordinary speed I finished polishing the other shoe. I put my shoes on without any socks because I had forgotten to wear any and there wasn't time to get them from under the bed. My mother appeared from the bathroom and called to me (apparently she wanted me to run some errand to the store) but I closed my ears and departed, unintentionally slamming the door behind me because my nerves were on edge.

I followed her, panting from excitement. My head was hunched down between my shoulders and the raised collar of my shirt because I was expecting my mother to call after me from the window of the parlour, but she didn't, thank God.

I fixed my eyes on Jasmine and began to devise such a blissful sexual union in my imagination that my forehead ran with sweat, even though it was a chilly morning; my blood was boiling with lust.

This wasn't an ordinary morning. Before I had walked behind Jasmine very far, some unruly boys chased me and began to throw stones at me. A short distance from there, dirty water spilled on my head from the downspout of an abandoned building. At a corner, a speeding car almost ran me down. When I was trying to cross a crowded street, a motorbike coming from the opposite direction hit me, threw me to the ground and scattered my books. My palms were scratched as they dragged along the pavement.

Despite these ill omens I resolved to follow Jasmine to our normal parting place where she turned left for the Faculty of Science and I turned right toward my secondary school. At that juncture I was overcome by a weird sensation of desolation. For the first time in my life I felt painful twinges in my heart. I stopped and turned back, following her with my eyes until she entered the gate and vanished.

That was the last time I saw her.

I spent a troubled day in the classroom where the teachers picked on me and scolded me. Even my classmates, who normally didn't act like this, made fun of me. I seemed to be inside a bubble that attracted other people's insults.

February 14th was the longest school day of my life; each class seemed as long as a whole academic year or more. I seemed to be carrying around some invisible weight. Chunks of stone, each weighing a ton, rested on my shoulders. By God, I almost died that day!

When the final bell rang I heaved a sigh of relief and raced off, happy to have ended my toughest school day. Anyone watching me would have been astonished and thought I was fleeing from a ghoul that wanted to rip me to shreds.

Once I neared our building I glanced at Jasmine's room. Then I noticed that the blue curtains were drawn and the window closed. I realized she hadn't returned from the university yet.

I ate a little rice and fish but didn't feel as hungry as usual; even my mother noticed and begged me to eat more. I rebuffed her brusquely and went to my room.

I wasn't able to concentrate on my homework: lines of text ran together and the books disgorged dreadful beasts. Lascivious female jinnis ran riot behind the pages.

A whistling wind whirled round in my brain and there was a bitter taste on my tongue. I stretched out on my bed and drew a cover over me.

I stroked my little friend but he didn't respond. Cursing him privately I withdrew my hand, which I placed as a pillow beneath my head, and dozed off. The afternoon call to prayer roused me and I went to the bathroom to wash. In the shower I remembered that I hadn't jerked off yet and stroked my tool again, vigorously, forcing him to obey my passions.

I know it's bad for my health to ejaculate when bathing but I wanted to take revenge on him and to vent my hostility against myself so I would feel better!

I dried off my body without touching my organ (that's what the jurisprudence instructor had taught us in order to retain our state of ritual purity) and performed the afternoon prayer hastily and distractedly. I don't know how many genuflections I performed. I don't even remember whether I eulogized the Prophet or not. What I do remember is daydreaming for some minutes and then standing up and folding the prayer rug.

I took 100 riyals from my mother and went down to Hajj Sultan's store. This wretch, who has grown more ill-tempered with the passing days, at first refused to serve me, coldly ignoring me as if I weren't there while a fly buzzed round the rim of the cup of *qishr*,[3] which he sucked through his decaying teeth.

I threatened to expose him in the community and to tell the adult men that he was shameless and pressed against girls and boys from the rear when they headed to the freezer for ice cream. His eyes grew red and he stormed with rage. He may have been tempted to pick up his cudgel and bash my head, but he had to factor in my father. So he meekly handed me what I had requested, even though he was puffing and shuddering like a viper.

---

3 *Qishr* is a Yemeni infusion made from coffee bean husks and spices

I settled down in my customary spot on the bench and looked up. Then I was thunderstruck to discover that her window was closed and her blinds down. This meant she wasn't in her room.

When she is there she raises the curtains and opens the window, which has a metal grille. When her spirit feels oppressed by the walls, she opens the grille, pokes her beautiful head out and looks right and left.

I thought I had come too late and that she had most probably left her room for a family visit or to attend a wedding. I stayed there till the sunset call to prayer. I went home, peed and did my ritual ablution. Then I performed the sunset prayer, ate a boiled potato and returned to my bench.

I looked at Jasmine's window and felt disappointed because her room was dark. Hunger gnawed at me and the cold stung me. All the same, I decided to remain resolutely in my spot until I obtained some sign that would reveal that Jasmine had returned safely to her throne. My heart was aching and I felt apprehensive.

At 8 p.m. my mother sent one of my little brothers to summon me to supper. I told him to tell Mother that I had dined. My hapless brother kept going up and down the stairs while I kept repeating the same response until my mother gave up on me.

A few minutes later, Salih, Jasmine's eldest brother, appeared wearing his military uniform and went upstairs to his family's apartment. Jasmine, who is the youngest child, has three older brothers. The eldest is Salih, whom I have just mentioned, the middle brother is Jamil and the youngest Hamdan. They have all enlisted in the armed services. Salih graduated from the War College and is now an officer with the rank of first lieutenant. Jamil graduated from the Air College and is now stationed at the military airport in al-Rub' al-Khali – the Empty Quarter. Hamdan is still a student at the War College.

Their father enrolled these three brothers in military service when they reached puberty at thirteen or fourteen so they would get used to a rough life and become accustomed to it. Later, they continued their education in different army camps. If women had been allowed to enlist, Hajj Nashir would probaby have forced his daughter into military service too.

The sound of wailing from the staircase of our building reached my ears. My chest quivered and I sensed that my nerves were tense with dread. I saw Jasmine's mother rush into the street covered in a Sanaa veil, sobbing and wailing. Jasmine's father and brother caught up with her and overpowered her, preventing her from running any further. Weeping feverishly she collapsed to the ground on her knees.

I felt my heart was in tatters and beating irregularly. The father and son were exchanging insults and abuse. From their screams I gathered that Salih held his father responsible for Jasmine's tardy return and contempt for the family's honour. Picking Jasmine's mother up by her arms they carried her back to the apartment.

Her words kept ringing in my ears, 'My daughter Jasmine is lost. Only God knows whether my daughter Jasmine is dead or alive. My daughter is off limits to you. Let me search for her. Let me go. Let me go!'

Cold sweat trickled down my limbs and I froze where I was, incredulous and thunderstruck. Jasmine's brother Hamdan, the student in the War College, arrived and bounded up the steps to the second floor.

Shortly thereafter two cars arrived. The first had a military plate and the second a civilian one. The two drivers remained in their vehicles. Moments later, the three men of the family had descended, leaving Jasmine's mother in the apartment by herself.

Salih rushed off in the military vehicle heading east, Hamdan and his father climbed into the other car and took off west. I thought I would go to the second floor to get the news about Jasmine straight from her mother. But I was too cowardly to take this step. Instead, I started to pace back and forth in front of the building's door, not knowing what to do.

At about 9 p.m. my father returned from his evening's work, scolded me for staying out this late and dragged me upstairs by my coat sleeve.

I went with him grudgingly and by the time we reached our apartment I was so anxious my guts were in knots. He lectured me for ten minutes that seemed like ten years to me, but fortunately his mobile phone rang. So he left me and retreated to the parlour, where he chatted and gabbled on and on.

I seized this opportunity and wrote a note on a scrap of paper to tell him I was going to search for the neighbour's lost daughter and wouldn't return until I found her. I asked my family not to worry about me.

I slipped away like a cat without anyone noticing. On the staircase I decided I would begin my search at the last place I had seen Jasmine heading for, the Faculty of Science.

I went out to the street where Hajj Sultan looked at me askance and followed me with his glances. At that moment I felt like hurling a rock at him and taking out his eye. I walked along quickly, examining every woman I passed as I told myself that perhaps this or that one was Jasmine.

When I reached the Faculty of Science I found its gate ajar. I shoved it a little and entered. There was no one at the guards' booth; they were inside watching television.

I inspected every inch of the faculty, even the restrooms, and looked inside the vehicles parked in the garage. I scaled the drainpipes to peer into the second-floor windows of the classrooms, the administrative offices and the library. I circled the buildings and went around the wall dozens of times but turned up nothing.

No one noticed I was there, although an inquisitive bird – I thought it was a hoopoe – kept following me from place to place. I headed to the garden and sat on a bench in a central location that allowed me to see in all directions.

I didn't feel tired but my feet hurt from six hours of nonstop walking. I removed my shoes and socks and stretched out on the bench. I looked up at the dome of the heavens where the stars were twinkling more brightly than usual and assuming meaningful geometric shapes. Do you suppose I just imagined it?

The hoopoe landed on the yellow grass and spread its royal crest. Then it began to dine on worms and larvae, ignoring my intrusion into its kingdom.

The gentle rustling of the trees in the night's still calm attracted my attention. What a sweet and delicate sound! Its music soothes the nerves. The garden was full of clamorous life, because insects and reptiles come out at night, when there are no people around, to search for a bite to eat and to get on with their lives.

An army of ants, crickets, beetles, grasshoppers, lizards, rats, moths, gnats and other flying pests whose names I don't know, inhabit the garden and create their evening world there. Who would believe this after the morning's light has dawned and people have made their way to this place? By this time, all those creatures, which fear men, will have hidden and taken refuge in their various resting places.

I heard footsteps on the ground. Trembling, I leapt to my feet and turned. Twenty steps away I noticed something that made me freeze with fear. Even my tongue felt so heavy it might have been made of iron.

I saw a clean-shaven man of medium build with a round face. Clad in an elegant suit of buttery beige, he wore white shoes and carried in his right hand a thick book with a white cover. He gazed at me steadily without moving. His look was filled with peace and love.

My fear of him gradually faded away. I felt relaxed and secure. I told myself, 'He seems to be one of the professors of the Faculty of Science, but the strange thing is, what brings him here at this late hour?'

He was watching my eyes silently as I raised my gaze toward him and then lowered it in order to memorize his shape and appearance, although the garden's meagre light wasn't much help. I thought the person standing before me was linked in some way to Jasmine's disappearance; at this point, doubts about him began to assail me. My suspicions reached the point that I thought he was mentally deranged and committed sadistic crimes against women. I imagined he had lured Jasmine to some isolated spot where he had strangled her. Then he had copulated with her corpse, which he had subsequently tossed into the boot of his car.

The man smiled as if he were reading my thoughts and took a few steps toward the pomegranate tree. Then he circled its trunk. I waited a whole minute for him to appear on the other side but he didn't.

I guessed he had hidden behind the tree trunk and shifted my position but couldn't see him. I called to him, 'Uncle! Uncle!' but he didn't reply. He had disappeared.

I approached the tree very slowly feeling terrified at the idea that I had seen a jinn. I'm a Muslim and the Holy Qur'an attests to the existence of the jinn. I recited to myself the Throne Verse from the Qur'an dozens of times while I walked forward at the speed of a tortoise. Then I recited it out loud in a low voice three times.

Finally, I summoned my courage and touched the tree trunk, praising God that it, at least, was real not imaginary. I walked round the tree a number of times and scrutinized its branches. It was inconceivable that he could have climbed the tree without my noticing.

I came to the conclusion that my recitation of the Throne Verse had incinerated the jinn. I patiently felt around the trunk, while my heart told me that something was waiting for me there. I discovered a crevice at the bottom of the trunk, approximately at ground level. My heart raced because the hole was dark and I'm instinctively afraid of reptiles and bugs.

The scaredy-cat lurking deep inside me began to warn me that venomous serpents might inhabit the cavity. I raised my head to look at the sky's face to appeal to it for help. Fortunately for me, a green shooting star appeared, splitting the dome of the heavens in two. I immediately felt better, as if the meteor had incinerated the coward inside me.

After saying 'bismillah' I poked my hand into the hole and my fingertips struck something. At first I was alarmed and drew my hand back. Then I renewed my attack and cautiously felt an object, which I grabbed and pulled out. It was a woman's black handbag. Looking at it carefully, I recognized it belonged to Jasmine. I moaned with delight and clutched the bag to my breast, kissing it and bringing it close to my nose to sniff. It still retained the fragrance of the perfume Jasmine invariably used.

I stretched out my hand and searched the hole again. I discovered something else, which I also pulled out. It was her notebook with the blue cover.

I don't know why but a strange feeling swept over me; the bag and notebook were presents from the man or jinn who had materialized in front of me; he had given them to me as a reward for my sincerity and perseverance in searching for the princess of hearts.

It suddenly occurred to me that the tree's spirit had shown itself to me in the guise of a human being. So I kissed the pomegranate tree to thank it for its gift.

Seizing my spoils I headed to the faculty exit. The guards were asleep and the gate was locked. I climbed its iron bars with ease and walked back toward my house.

No one saw me. The streets were deserted, just a few dogs barking in the distance.

Halfway home, loudspeakers suddenly split the air with the call to the dawn prayer. I realized it was 4.30 a.m. and quickened my pace to avoid running into people setting off early to perform their prayers in the mosques.

The whole way home, suspended in the void before me, I imagined an ancient wooden door with an iron knocker on which Jasmine's face was embossed. I wondered whether this door would open, where it led to, where it came from and what my relationship to it was.

I was so tired when I reached home that I almost collapsed on the ground, but the door to the building was closed. I pressed the intercom button and my mother answered. I asked her to come down and let me in. I heard a din I couldn't understand and then she hung up.

My father opened the door, his face glowering. He jerked me by the collar of my coat and hoisted me up, even though I'm heavy. I walked up two steps and then sailed through the air over the third.

My weeping mother greeted and embraced me to protect me from the anticipated punishment. My father brought out a knotted electric cord and prepared to beat me with it. I pulled Jasmine's bag and notebook from under my coat and threw them on the ground.

My father, whose eyelids were dark from his night's vigil and from rage, asked me, 'Dog, what's this?'

Raising my arms to ward off any blow I replied, 'This is Jasmine's handbag and that's her course notebook.'

My mother groaned in alarm, but my father's mouth fell open. He didn't say a word. He went pale and his pupils began to revolve in his eyes in a way that made me pity him.

I picked up Jasmine's belongings and retreated to my room where I stretched out on my bed without removing my clothes or shoes. I placed the bag and notebook under my pillow.

They followed me and sat on the edge of the bed. My father tried to discover how I had acquired these two items, where I had found them and why I had brought them home.

His questions came in quick succession but a thick fog enveloped me and in only a few seconds I lost first my ability to hear and then the rest of my senses. My eyelids closed and I sailed away on the ship of sleep, surfing as many dreams as there are stars.

5
The Sceptic whose Scepticism Disappears Like a Scattering Cloud

At noon on February 19th we arrested the individual known as Ali Nashwan on his return from school. Inspector Abdurrabbih and I were in an unmarked car. We stopped him in the al-Qaʿ neighbourhood and asked him to climb into the vehicle. He obeyed without any objection. We took him to the Criminal Investigations Headquarters and interrogated him.

My name is Mutiʿ Radman and I'm a police officer with the rank of Deputy Inspector. I work with Inspector Abdurrabbih, assisting him in the field and writing up reports of investigations for him.

Ali is an adolescent of average intelligence; naïve. His eyes are almond-shaped and frank, and his mouth is small and pursed. His lips are rose-red and firm. He has bushy eyebrows and on his left cheek a broad scar extends from his cheekbone to below his earlobe, but this memento from a past fight doesn't detract from his handsome appearance.

When we asked how he had acquired Jasmine's handbag and course notebook he told us a long and incredible tale. He said that a jinn wearing an extremely chic modern suit had given him the bag and notebook. His words were disjointed and confused. He would stutter, run words together and occasionally start babbling. Then we were forced to comfort him, stroke his head and give him a glass of water to clear his throat.

He is a pampered boy who is afraid of his own shadow. Over and beyond all this he was perspiring profusely and smelled bad. I fully expected Inspector Abdurrabbih to command me to take him to the electric room and shock him to loosen his tongue so he would confess the truth. He was definitely lying. His statements wouldn't deceive a child. It was clear he was embroiled in something momentous. His conduct proved he knew a lot he didn't want to reveal. Surprisingly enough, Inspector Abdurrabbih ordered him set free! Perhaps he took pity on him because he's a minor.

I broached the topic with him while we were chewing *qat* in a *qat* den and he replied that imprisoning Ali wouldn't help us at all and that the best thing would be to keep track of his movements and contacts because he was the thread that would lead us to the missing Jasmine.

We served Dr. Aqlan with an official summons but he didn't respond. Then I telephoned him and informed him that we were expecting him to appear at such-and-such a time. He repeated his pompous refusal to obey and hung up on me. We can't get back at him because he has influential connections in the government. If we try to show him our fangs he'll fall upon us with his talons and hurl us beyond the sun.

We went to his office in the Faculty of Science calculating the time carefully to prevent him from escaping on the pretext of one or another of his lectures. He proffered us a smile several kilometres wide and a hand as cold as a corpse. Without his noticing it I turned on my mobile phone to record his statements. His attention was focused on Inspector Abdurrabbih.

We emerged with extremely important information. He had seen the same man Ali had told us about. I was astonished at how closely the descriptions matched. So the boy hadn't been inventing fantastic things from his imagination.

Dr. Aqlan said that through his window he had seen Jasmine sitting with a mature man who had a handsome face, which was clean shaven, and that the sun had tanned his skin till it was almost the colour of gazelle's blood. He wore an expensive light brown suit with a white shirt and his gold necktie had red stripes.

He made a curious observation, saying that al-Utmi, the proprietor of the snack bar, had gestured cryptically to that man, who had then shown him a book bound in gleaming white paper.

I expected Inspector Abdurrabbih to inquire about the rumours that the professor had failed Jasmine in his subject to force her to come to his residence. He himself had been expecting that question and for this reason remained tense, answering us with terse replies and in a hostile, haughty tone.

Inspector Abdurrabbih didn't dare ask because the man has support from above. Any faux pas might bring down upon us a stern reckoning; in the final analysis we're nothing more than low-ranking policemen who lack any clout or power.

We said goodbye to him, thanking him for graciously answering our questions and departed, praising God for our safe deliverance, as if he were the one who had been interrogating us, not the other way around.

Who was this adult male three people had already seen?

We asked the forensic lab's artist to prepare a composite sketch of that mysterious middle-aged man based on the descriptions furnished by Dr. Aqlan, Ali Nashwan and al-Utmi, the snack bar proprietor.

We showed the composite drawing to the three of them and altered it to match as far as possible the image imprinted in their memories. Then we distributed the man's picture to all the other police departments and squads and issued both an all-points bulletin for his arrest and a travel prohibition for him at any border crossing, airport or seaport.

We searched for Jasmine in all of Yemen's provinces and achieved nothing. It seemed that a sorceress had turned her into a mare! We received the bodies of unidentified women but none of them matched her description.

We assigned detectives in shifts to monitor the garden of the Faculty of Science twenty-four hours a day and provided them with mobile phones with cameras, charging that to the agency.

Jasmine's tribe was pressuring us and complicating our work. Dozens of armed men flocked to the station to inquire about the latest news. I don't know how the picture of the unidentified, middle-aged man was leaked to them but they began to search for him, threatening him with a hideous death.

Toward the end of February, the case began to take on tragic dimensions; events were heading in a violent and bloody direction but all we could do was shrug our shoulders and wiggle our hips.

Our scouts scattered through the Faculty of Science advised us that Ali Nashwan never left the garden, not even at night. The university guards would encircle him at sunset and expel him by force, securely locking the gate, but he would secretly scale the wall and spend the whole night by the pomegranate tree. In the morning they would find him clasping the tree's trunk, snoring in his sleep like a contented cow.

We kept him under surveillance overnight and found that he spent the whole time in worship. He would pray facing the pomegranate tree. Had he lost his mind? Was he well on his way to insanity? We didn't know what was transpiring in his weak, childish brain.

The inquiries we made about him indicated that Ali Nashwan was rather pious and keen on performing the five daily prayers at the right times. The clique he hung out with was made up of religiously committed young men.

Unbeknownst to him, we photographed him kneeling in prayer and prostrating himself before the tree. He would also embrace its trunk and kiss it reverently and respectfully. He circumambulated it submissively and piously while mumbling arcane, incomprehensible words, which our translators failed to recognize as belonging to any known language.

I clapped my hands together; Ali Nashwan, the upright, prayerful boy had become a heathen!

On the night of February 27th something weird happened, something we're unable to explain logically. The problem was that our surveillance of Ali Nashwan grew a little slack when the agent tailing him succumbed to a peaceful sleep. When his replacement arrived at 2 a.m. he found the garden empty; there was no trace of Ali Nashwan, who had departed and passed through the faculty gate without anyone noticing.

The only person to provide us with useful information about him was the night watchman stationed at a corner from which he could see people entering and leaving the apartment building inhabited by Jasmine's and Ali's families. This agent mentioned that around 1 a.m. he saw Ali Nashwan open the building's door and enter; he had also noticed that Ali was hiding something under his overcoat.

We weren't able to exploit this valuable piece of information because we dawdled and arrived after it was too late. The next day Ali Nashwan was missing too, and his family began searching for him. We, for our part, wanted him to help solve the riddles into which he had plunged us. But neither we nor his family were able to locate him.

On March 10th, we received a report that a boy's body had been found in one of Sanaa's suburbs. Inspector Abdurrabbih sent me to investigate, accompanied by a medical examiner and a photographer.

Three police vehicles had already arrived at the scene and policemen had formed a ring to prevent curious onlookers from coming too close. When one of the policemen pulled away the black army blanket, I immediately recognized the corpse of Ali Nashwan. I contacted Inspector Abdurrabbih and informed him of developments.

After a quick preliminary examination the medical examiner affirmed that the cause of death had been extreme torture. Ali Nashwan's face was swollen and covered with wounds. There were contusions on his head, his bones were broken and crushed, and his ribcage had been completely demolished. His male organ had been chopped off and his groin area had been stabbed repeatedly. Tucked between his buttocks was a wilted bouquet of *qat*.

When Inspector Abdurrabbih joined us he was glowering and there were tears in his eyes. He may have felt the pangs of conscience for releasing Ali Nashwan. I also privately blamed him.

We devoted six hours to examining the site and searching for clues. All the same, we turned up nothing of value.

The suburb consists of repulsive-looking, rocky hills on which stand a few, widely spaced houses. The whole area is forlorn and desolate. It is reached by a winding dirt road that falls and rises as if a person were travelling through the land of the jinn.

Once we had completed our procedures we delivered Ali's body to his family, who held an abbreviated funeral that lasted only a day. Then they buried him. A few days later, Ali's mother died of sorrow and grief over the loss of her eldest son.

The case grew more complicated by the day. Jasmine had already been missing for a month and we had been unable to gain any information about her whereabouts. In the meantime, we had been responsible for the blood of a victim murdered in the prime of his youth. As for the unidentified, middle-aged man dressed like a foppish bridegroom, we had grown dizzy trying to determine his whereabouts. We virtually died of fatigue while attempting to discover his name and identity. No one the length and breadth of Yemen matched the composite portrait of him!

In the end, I personally became convinced that he wasn't human. He was one of those jinn who love to play with our nerves.

Now I'm trying to erase his image from my imagination. Whenever I think of him I feel my spirit is fluttering, attempting to free itself from my body. Was he Azrael, the angel of death, in disguise? I've seen hundreds of mutilated corpses – lacerated, dismembered and mangled – without that ruffling a single hair of my body, but the image of this unidentified middle-aged man is driving me crazy. He passes before my eyes all the time, even in my dreams!

I don't know any reason for this persistence, for this overwhelming presence. Occasionally I see his shadow on walls. At other times, when I'm walking I notice a puddle of silver water that undulates and emits a blinding gleam.

A glowing light follows me everywhere, almost as if something wanted to materialize before me, to emerge from its numinous world into my visible one. I don't like these supernatural apparitions. I hate them intensely. I fear that I'm losing my mental equilibrium and that I'll find myself racing through the streets with my privates uncovered while I preach to the thin air.

I consulted a shaykh who treats people with the Qur'an. He recited the Qur'anic sura 'Ya-Sin' over some water, which absorbed the words with his breath. Then he handed this to me, telling me to take a sip each time I finished praying for the next thirty days. He also cautioned me against eating onions or garlic and told me not to sleep on my stomach.

So now I'm trying to cure myself of these sick imaginings.

6
The Ascetic

When locusts attacked Sanaa, children and adults went out to collect them alive in empty metal water buckets. I gave my daughter Jasmine a clean water bucket and she descended delightedly to the street, setting off with her little girl friends to collect locusts, bounding after them.

I asked her to do that because I felt like eating some. We sauté them with a little salt and they make a delicious, nutritious dish. A few people eat them live without salt.

Salma, the metalworker's daughter, brought a light plastic ball. So the girls put the buckets aside and began to play football. They may have played for as long as twenty minutes before they tired and returned to their homes. But my husband, may God forgive him, had a fit, blew everything out of proportion, and turned it into a huge issue.

Following this incident, he forced Jasmine to wear the *niqab*, prevented her from playing in the street and forbade her to associate with any males who are not part of the family group.

My name is Wahiba. I've borne three sons and one daughter and suffered seven miscarriages.

Jasmine began to write a diary after she was secluded and her movements were restricted. That notebook became her consolation in her wretched isolation. She was quite concerned that no one should look at her diary so she thrust it in a locked drawer and always kept the key with her.

For my part, I respected her privacy and saw nothing wrong with her keeping her secrets. I felt confident about my daughter's conduct and had absolutely no doubts about her purity because I'm the one who raised her and her brothers. I know that she's superior to them culturally and morally.

It definitely never crossed my mind to steal a look at her diary, even though I had my own key to the drawer. She didn't know that. I'm a woman who had an honourable, rural upbringing. That's why I think it's wrong to look at things the owner has shielded from prying eyes.

A year after Jasmine disappeared, when I had totally despaired of her ever returning, my longing for her tempted me to open her drawer and to take out her fancy diary, which has a leather binding. My feeling of loss prompted me to seek consolation in reading what her pen had written.

I wasn't disappointed; she had recorded her feelings and her opinions about the people around her on the brown, burnished paper. She said of me that I'm a woman obsessed by cleanliness and hostility to spiders and their webs, and that the smallest amount of dust in the house makes me gasp for breath and inflames my eyelids. I admit this is true.

She said that I worry about what people say, fear their envy and believe in the evil eye and the harm it causes. That's why I burn incense in the apartment every day and hang Qur'anic verses in each of the rooms and hallways.

She mentioned that I favour her brothers over her. (This isn't true, I swear.) She described me as an affectionate, tender mother when pleased and a stern, harsh one when angry.

She said that she loves me more than she loves herself and expressed her love for me in hundreds of places. Each time I read this, tears streamed down my cheeks.

She said that her father is gruff and mean-spirited on the outside but that deep inside he is good and generous. She said he is forced to adopt an exterior like that of a hedgehog with sharp, defensive quills because society respects a man whose behaviour is belligerent and petulant and mocks a man who is complacent and chaste in expression. She said he is an ignorant, domineering father but that in spite of his many faults she loves him dearly.

She mentioned many of our male and female neighbours and recorded her memories of them. Her diary revealed some things I hadn't known. For example, the shopkeeper Hajj Sultan used to flirt with her!

What Jasmine recorded corroborates the rumour that women in the neighbourhood have spread about him. The substance of it is that Afiya, a poor but beautiful widow with six orphaned children to support, receives food from him to feed her children and then, when no one is looking, slips into the shop's stockroom to settle her accounts!

She mentioned our neighbour's son Ali in her diary more than seventy times. Ali is like a son to me. At first we were on intimate terms with him and had our own pet name for him: sweet Ali. When I remember this charming boy I sigh because we wronged him. We killed him, even though he was innocent. I still have a photo of him (I don't remember now how I got it) and whenever I look at it my eyes flow with tears of regret and remorse.

When I'm all alone by the trunk of the pomegranate tree, I occasionally recall the way the doorbell rang continually at 1 a.m. one morning. That was ten days after Jasmine had disappeared. When we opened the door, Ali entered, breathless, his face beaming with joy and delight. He handed us all the clothes that my lost daughter had been wearing, including her underclothes.

We asked him roughly where he had obtained these garments. Then he told us a strange story. He said he had gone to search for Jasmine in the Faculty of Science. In the garden, near a pomegranate tree, he had seen a medium-height, middle-aged man wearing white clothes with a golden gleam and holding a luminous white book. He had looked carefully at Ali and then disappeared. When Ali had approached the tree he had found a crevice in its trunk. Then he had stuck in his hand and had pulled out Jasmine's handbag and course notebook.

When my son Jamil, who had just arrived from Hadramawt, asked why Ali hadn't delivered those items to us, he replied that his father had given them the next day to Inspector Abdurrabbih and that they were now in the custody of Criminal Investigations.

We encouraged him to continue and he said that after his success in retrieving Jasmine's bag and notebook he had begun to hover around the pomegranate tree. Then he had started chanting in some foreign tongue, although he didn't understand a single word of it. He had felt the presence of spirits around him and for a while lights shone. He kept doing all this until the man of medium build appeared once more. The man opened the white book and turned its pages as if inviting him to read. When he looked he realized that it was written in an alphabet he didn't know. Then the man pointed to a crevice in the trunk and vanished as if he had never been there. So he stuck his hand in and pulled out a pile of cloth. When he examined this he recognized it as our lost daughter's clothing. So he shoved everything under his coat and rushed to us.

None of us, neither I, nor my husband, nor my three sons, believed a word he said. So we thought the worst of him. My son Hamdan raised his *janbiya* dagger and threatened him: 'You've brought us our sister's clothes, even her bra, so tell us where she is or I'll kill you with my own hands the way I would slaughter a lamb.'

Ali collapsed in tears and proceeded to swear weighty oaths that he was telling the truth.

My son Salih struck him and dragged him by his hair, demanding that he tell the truth. We were all shouting in his face like madmen, raising our voices at that late hour of the night. Before the neighbours could gather to see why we were screaming, my husband intervened and threw Ali out of the house. My husband and three sons immediately headed to the residence of our tribe's shaykh and told him what had happened. With their consent the shaykh initiated a vile conspiracy.

When Ali left the building on his way to school, armed men from our tribe intercepted him on one of the streets and forced him at gunpoint to climb into the car with them. They took him to the shaykh's private prison where they tortured and beat him to make him tell the truth and show them where Jasmine had fled. But he didn't change a single word of his claims before departing from this life, may God be compassionate to his soul!

Whenever the shaykh has met me he has maligned my daughter's reputation, saying, 'Your daughter's a whore who ran away with some guy who took her fancy.' I always start sobbing and defend my daughter's honour under my breath whenever I hear that damaging statement of his.

The men of our tribe boasted about their crimes against Ali; details such as their crushing his bones with rifle butts, slicing off his penis, pounding his head against the walls and stabbing him below his belly spread through all the households of the neighbourhood until the news reached the ears of our neighbour Umm Ali. Then her heart swelled up and she died only a few days after her son was slain.

I was afraid my husband and sons would be arrested and put on trial, but the shaykh's influence shielded them from interrogation. Inspector Abdurrabbih and all the top brass of Criminal Investigations were fully briefed on the details of the crime because these were common knowledge but they refrained from apprehending the killers, preferring to keep the peace. Any accusation against the criminals who shed Ali's blood would be an accusation against the entire tribe; neither Inspector Abdurrabbih nor anyone else was ready to start a confrontation with our tribe.

No one dared to seek revenge for Ali's murder, not the state, not even his family; it seemed that shedding his blood was permissible, as if it were a dog's blood.

After heads had cooled and the men of our tribe felt that they had restored its honour and prestige by killing that little boy, the shaykh came up with the idea of visiting a famous clairvoyant in Qaʿ Jahran to ask him where Jasmine was. After hearing Jasmine's story from start to finish, he asked them to give him till the next day. My husband placed 100,000 riyals in the clairvoyant's lap, requesting that he ask the jinn who assisted him to discover Jasmine's whereabouts before nightfall. The man took our money and disappeared into a darkened room for an hour. With these two eyes of mine I saw the stones of the building where he met with the jinn quake and emit a heart-stopping roar.

When he emerged, dripping with sweat, his eyes gleamed in an odd way and he told us that Jasmine had been abducted by an intrepid *afreet* who had manifested himself to her in the form of a handsome bridegroom. He had seen her in the land of the jinn, where she was a slave in a palace of *afreets*. She was cooking, washing and sweeping. She craved certain foods because the vicious jinn had raped her and made her pregnant.

My husband's face darkened in response to this alarming news and he passed out. His honour had been lost, once and for all. His daughter was pregnant, and with what? She was pregnant with a jinn!

My three sons were furious and begged the clairvoyant to show them how to redeem their sister and free her from slavery. The shaykh, swept up by tribal chauvinism, swore by his grandfathers that he would crush the *afreet*'s bones and castrate him!

The clairvoyant told them they should go to the pomegranate tree that had abducted Jasmine because the *afreet*'s homeland was within it. He asked them to command the *afreet* to return the human being, whose family he had wronged by taking her, exactly the way she was when he seized her, sound of mind and body without any addition or deletion. Otherwise they would incinerate him.

He ordered them to address the culprit for three consecutive days. If he responded and returned the girl they should leave him alone. If he did not yield, they wouldn't be blamed for burning down the pomegranate tree.

The men of our tribe swallowed this nonsense and believed the lie of the clairvoyant, who was laughing up his sleeve at their ignorance. Armed with rifles and machine guns they stationed themselves for three days and nights by the pomegranate tree, alarming and terrifying the students.

On the fourth day they cut down the pomegranate tree, dividing the wood between them to use as firewood for their outdoor ovens. Naturally, my daughter didn't return to my embrace, nor was the alleged rebel jinn consumed by flames. All that happened was that the men of our tribe washed their hands of my daughter's disappearance after this foolish exorcism. By burning her alive along with her abductor they wiped out the dishonour she had caused.

We gave all the money we had to that quack to find some stratagem to allow us to paper over this scandal. Thus a story was pieced together (stitched with a cudgel rather than a needle) to allow us to explain away the loss of our daughter and hold up our heads before other people.

All the same, the puzzle of her disappearance wasn't resolved. Where has Jasmine gone? What is she doing now do you suppose? Is she alive or dead? These questions continued to keep me awake at night, knotting my stomach and mauling my flesh.

I was ready to sacrifice my very life to anyone who would tell me a single word about her, but my reading of her diary later opened a possibility that had absolutely not occurred to me. There were revelatory hints in her diary, signs that pointed out the path I needed to follow in order to reach her.

I bathed, performed my ablutions, burned incense and put on clean clothes. Then I headed to the Faculty of Science bringing a bottle of perfume with me. I searched in its garden for any trace of its pomegranate tree but to no avail. I rushed over to a grey-haired man working in a nearby snack bar and asked for his help. He accompanied me into the garden while checking me out. Then he pointed to a stump that had a cavity at the bottom. He told me, 'This is what remains of the pomegranate tree.'

I thanked him and he turned to go back to work. For my part, I poured the perfume over the trunk and spread it all over it. Then I sat down to contemplate it, sitting still and motionless.

From that day till now this has become a daily habit: I visit the tree trunk and anoint it with perfume each morning, because for me it has become tantamount to my missing daughter's tomb. This trunk has become the shelter for my memories, the resting place of my tears, the companion for my solitude and the balm of my sorrows.

The trunk is no longer a dead stump. Instead, it is the umbilical cord that connects me to Jasmine. I've become her foetus and seek a new birth through her womb.

The middle-aged man whom Ali of blessed memory twice saw dressed like a bridegroom was someone my daughter Jasmine had met in her dreams. He used to visit her almost every night.

In her diary I found a detailed record of those visions. Taken as a whole these dreams contained happy encounters! She wrote that she would wake up intoxicated even though she would feel every part of her body to make sure she hadn't lost any.

The last thing she recorded in her diary was this extremely odd dream that did not resemble her other dreams at all. It was more like a prophecy of what would happen to her on the morning of February 14th, the day she disappeared from this world.

> I dreamt I was in the Faculty of Science listening to a lecture by Dr. Ajlan. Then I left, by myself, and headed to the snack bar where I handed Uncle Nasir al-Utmi a sprig of basil. I entered the girls' area, ate, drank and laughed with my girlfriends. Then I left them and walked into the garden where I relaxed on the bench next to the pomegranate tree. I began laughing for no reason at all. I removed all my clothes, stripped naked and then stretched out on the bench. I started to sing out loud and the turtledove repeated the refrain as if it were a choir.
>
> My singing was interrupted by the appearance of the man who claims he is my bridegroom. When I sat up and covered my privates with my hand he sat down opposite me.
>
> He didn't say a word and kept looking at my eyes as if he were the Angel of Death pursuing one of his victims.
>
> I broke the barrier of silence and fear. 'I've seen you in my dreams,' I told him, turning for fear one of the men or women students would hear my strange confession.
>
> He smiled in a mysterious way that increased my confusion and my fear of him.
>
> 'I believe I possess a knack for truly discerning what is passing through other people's souls by reading their eyes,' I said while looking in his eyes and swallowing with difficulty.
>
> 'That's a lovely claim; what are my eyes telling you now?' he asked while I felt his eyes pierce me and penetrate my innermost spirit.
>
> 'They tell me that you're not a human being like us,' I said while my eyes squinted violently and my pupils hurt from looking at him, as if I were looking at the eye of the Sun.
>
> He turned his eyes away toward the horizon, and did not reply.

I asked him cautiously with awe, 'Who are you?'

After some reflection he replied, 'I am knowledge's goal that rests in the hearts of all.'

His answer shocked me and I fell silent.

He began to read a book that had no title and that was bound in lustrous white paper. Meanwhile I was busy contemplating him and remembering my dreams about him.

Suddenly I found myself wresting the white book from his hand – just like that without any premeditation – and trying to read it. I was stricken by a violent fright and asked, 'What's this? The book has no writing in it. What were you reading?'

He laughed sedately and retrieved his book saying, 'You golden daisy, all books revealed before their time lack writing. Haven't you noticed that?'

I stood up, annoyed by his riddles. Pointing a trembling finger at him I said awkwardly, 'You're a sorcerer!'

He gestured for me to sit down and be calm to avoid attracting the other students' attention. He told me in an affectionate tone, 'O Crowned Queen of Hearts, here is the book. Look. It actually is a book without any writing in it. Where's the sorcery in this? What's so strange about that?'

Feeling very tense I sat down. My whole body was trembling with emotion. Uncle Nasir al-Utmi, the snack bar proprietor, noticed my confusion and discomfort and waved to me encouragingly. I thanked him with all my heart for this gesture, because it made me feel I still belonged to this world.

The man who claimed to be my bridegroom began to thumb through the white book again, deliberately ignoring me. I watched him for a time as he read aloud, mumbling incomprehensible words.

'What do you want from me?' I asked entreatingly as tears flowed from my eyes.

'I want to realize your dearest dreams,' he replied nonchalantly, thereby determining my destiny.

Lost in thought I began to recall the dream I had every night. I would see this man, who claimed he was my bridegroom, open the locked door of my room. Then he would enter and close the door as if zipping up a pair of trousers. He looked at me lying on the bed as naked as when my mother brought me into the world. The room's only illumination slid dimly through the window from the lights in the street.

He approached, embracing me with his eyes. Then he began to circle me holding a sparkling white book and reciting under his breath. Eventually I sensed that waves of delight were flowing into me as I felt sexual gratification flood from my head to my feet time and again. Each wave of erotic delight was twice as strong and forceful as the previous one. I was the only female in existence and all males in existence were penetrating me. I felt an electric pleasure that surpassed anything imaginable. I sensed that the phalluses of billions of men were ejaculating into my vagina simultaneously as I climaxed along with all of them. I felt their strong arms squeeze me and massage every point on my body. Then I disintegrated into the powdery colours of a rainbow sprayed by winds among the clouds. At one moment I felt I was a cloud as lightning stormed into me, affording me terrifying pleasure. At another time I felt I was the earth comforted by the Sun's rays' delicate bliss. At the climactic moment, I sensed I was the universe; the billions of stars generated inside me were embryos being created in my womb. Ultimately I experienced a pure pleasure no human being has ever known, and then the window of my mind opened once more on ordinary life.

When I woke, I was flushed and glowing.

Returning to my senses, I noticed that the man who claimed to be my bridegroom had risen and begun to circle me, his white book open in his hands. He was reciting from it, chanting sounds I had never heard before.

My body began to perspire, I blanched as blood drained from my veins, and my throat suddenly felt parched.

I lost the ability to move the parts of my body, although my eyes were revolving crazily in their sockets.

I experienced a profound delight as I dissolved through an ecstasy of love into an existence that outstrips words and into a presence that defies logic.

I grew very light as the space I once occupied in this world dwindled away.

Where was I? I don't know. But I was boundlessly happy.

I still had the ability to see.

The person who claims he is my bridegroom sat down on the bench and his face reflected an indescribable inner happiness.

Uncle Nasir al-Utmi, the snack bar proprietor, noticed that I had disappeared suspiciously and that the man dressed as a bridegroom was sitting there alone. So Uncle Nasir waggled his hand and winked as he asked, 'Where's the girl gone?'

The person claiming to be my bridegroom rose and pointed to the white book as he turned its pages.

Uncle Nasir al-Utmi scratched his head, puzzled that the man should show him a book like any other filled with writing.